CAPTIVATING
COMMANDER

CAPTIVATING COMMANDER

A Cocky Hero Club World Novel
International Bestselling Author
Tiffany Carby

Editor: Ann Atwood

Cover Design: Whiskers & Whimsy Designs

Formatting: By Quill & Lantern

Photo Credit: Depositphotos

CONTENTS

To my sister, for always being more.

INTRODUCTION

Captivating Commander is a standalone story inspired by Vi Keeland and Penelope Ward's *Playboy Pilot*. It's published as part of the Cocky Hero Club world, a series of original works, written by various authors, and inspired by Keeland and Ward's *New York Times* bestselling series.

CHAPTER ONE

Lay. Over. Or shall I say, *laid* over?

It didn't take long for me to fly into the hotshot playboy pilot wings I was destined to wear. No, siree.

Spending a couple of rookie years really learning the ins and outs of pilothood, I made sure to take it slow and easy with the ladies, as I honed my skills and learned from the masters before me. Specifically, my mentor, Carter Clynes, who had since retired from commercial pilotdom and left the *laying over* to the rest of us.

I missed my old buddy, especially the times we spent behind the wheels of a 747. He was almost always commander of a flight when we were together. I think I only remembered one time we flew together that I took point, and it was because he was a fill-in. That whole flight I was nervous I'd let him down. I was also an *idiot*. I knew my planes inside and out, and could fly in my sleep. But, of course, I wouldn't.

Meeting Trip and the guys for a bachelor party on a layover in Boca was just the kind of R&R I needed.

"Long time no see, man," Trip said, welcoming me to the bar with a cold beer in one hand and our *secret pilot handshake* that made me feel like a young wingman again.

"Twerrrrp!" we said simultaneously, as we turned the imaginary wheel and bumped fists.

"Bah, I can't believe we still remember that," he read my mind. After a large gulp of ice-cold beer, Trip introduced me to some other pilots that I didn't know, and I got reacquainted with a few I did.

"Where's the man of the hour?" I asked, after getting settled at the swanky old establishment. The large high-top table seated us all with room for more, and sat off to the side of the bar for a little added privacy. It felt a little mob-like with all the wood decor and dim lighting. There were plenty of single ladies perusing around the pilots as well. All those silver wings shining on the collars around our table got their attention. I didn't mind using my profession to pick up girls. Why not, right? I earned those wings.

"Just got a text and he's on his way, delayed, of course," one of the pilots told the table.

Trip and I were able to catch up, and I was pleased to hear he was enjoying his new *family lifestyle*.

"Definitely miss flying with you, but I'm happy you're happy," I told him. A new round of drinks appeared one after the other, until I wasn't even sure which round we were on. "So, Kendall and Brucey are good? And you're enjoying your new gig?"

"They are and I am, life is fine, man," he said. "When are you gonna settle down, Dawx?"

"Heh, yeah, right, I'm enjoying the ways of the *playboy pilot* a little too much to even think about a long-term relationship." I raised my glass as the others chimed in and cheered to being the players we were.

"Old Trip here is the sell-out, settling down and leaving the ways!" one of the others hollered, from the opposite end of the table.

"Ah, you guys, hush, I've never been happier," he said. One of the ladies who kept floating around our table came up behind Trip, as he was telling the guys how much he loved his wife. She grimaced and backed up, noticing the silver band on his ring finger. I couldn't help but laugh. Trip used to be the most popular of our crowd with the ladies. I always enjoyed watching the birds flock to him and seeing what he did with them. It was a long time since Trip had been in action and I hated to see a lady suffer from his unavailability.

"Hi," I got up and said to the wounded bird. I held up my hand. "No ring on this finger."

"Oh, you're a Captain Obvious, are ya?" she snarked back.

"Commander Obvious has a nicer ring to it, don't you think?" I turned the corner of my smile into a smirk and winked. "Buy you a drink?"

She accepted my offer and I followed her to the end of the bar. The tight skirt she wore was shorter than most mamas would approve of, but I didn't mind. It hugged all the right curves.

Need a place to stay tonight? Trip sent me a text as I was flirting with the bird.

If all goes well with this one, nope! I figured I'd find someone to go home with, at least for one night, and could figure the housing out for the rest of my layover later.

She ordered a beer, which was fine by me, because beer was cheap, but also told me she either drank a lot, or didn't know what she liked to order. The longer we talked, the more I realized she hung around this particular bar because

3

of the pilots that would frequent the place. It was close to the airport and near the hotels where flight staff would stay on layovers. I knew her type and she knew mine. No shame in seeing one for what they were.

"My name is Diamond," she finally said. "I see your last name on your tag, but I'm not even gonna try to pronounce it."

I looked down and realized I hadn't taken my nametag off. Several of us hadn't after I looked back to our group. I usually did when I unbuttoned the top of my shirt since I wasn't technically in uniform, but apparently got carried away with the reunion today.

"Sorry about that, I'm Dawson, and my last name is pronounced Kaa-ja-mar-eck...Dawson Kaczmarek."

"That is a mouthful," she said. Not the first time I had heard that one either.

"I've been told *I'm a mouthful* a time or two," I said, but couldn't keep a straight face.

"Oh, have you, Dawson?"

"Mmm-hmm... and you can call me Dawx, if you want. It's been my nickname since college."

"Dawx... I like that... you'll have to tell me the story behind that nickname."

"Maybe later," I cut her off with a wink. That wasn't a getting-to-know-you conversation. At least, not in this scenario.

"Well, my friends call me Diamond," she said, and giggled just as the door swung open and Everett, the bachelor in question, walked in.

"I'm gonna have to go hang out with these guys for a bit, but if you plan on staying around, maybe we can chat more later?" I asked, knowing she got my drift.

"Yeah, sure, I'll be around for a while," she said and blew me a kiss.

I suddenly had plans for Diamond...

"All really great flying
adventures begin at dawn."

- Stephen Coonts

CHAPTER TWO

"For he's a jolly good fellow," they slurred. I couldn't believe people still sang that song, but too many beers and tradition came out in full force, and these pilots were drunker than skunks. Apparently, I held my liquor a little better than the rest of them.

As the celebration of our bachelor started winding down, I told Trip we had to have one more drink before he left, anxious to get back to his wife before it got too late.

"She knows this is a bachelor party, dude," I reminded him.

"Yes, and I'm ready to go home to her," he said, grinning like a cat. "It's a whole new ballgame having someone waiting on you, instead of always fishing. I mean it, man, when you find the one, you'll see it too."

"A couple shots of bourbon," I ordered, and I noticed Diamond making her way back down the bar to my side.

"Bourbon, eh?" Trip asked. "Going out with a bang?"

"I'm far from done, but I know you're gonna bail on me so..." The bartender set two glasses on the bar and we tossed them back.

"So, introduce me to your married friend," Diamond said, as she put her hand on my shoulder.

"Diamond, this is Carter, an old pilot buddy of mine," I said.

He held out his hand to shake hers. Her hand behaved like a dead fish when she plopped her fingers in his. You could tell a lot about a person's handshake.

"Aye, Diamond, why don't you come over here and show a little love to me and my buddies, leave these preppies to their drinks?" a big guy in a leather vest hollered at her, as a few of his friends catcalled to get her attention.

I looked over and saw they were going to continue.

"Don't worry about Bruno. He doesn't know how to take no for an answer," she said, turning my attention back to her and her low-cut blue blouse.

"Hey, Diamond! I wasn't kidding! We're regulars here and they're just flybys!" he taunted, and I knew I was going to have to put a stop to this. The longer I knew Diamond, the sleazier she became, and I was seriously considering just crashing at Trip's place and bailing on her. But, something in me wouldn't allow Bruno to continue to demean her, regardless of my intentions for the rest of the evening.

"Leave her alone, man," I said over her shoulder, and noticed Trip was giving me a look.

"Not worth it," he said under his breath, and laid his glass down for the bartender to refill it.

Bruno was suddenly at my back and I was aggravated.

"Whatcha gonna do about it, pretty boy?" he said in my ear. I swiftly turned and suggested we take it outside, so I could *explain it to him*.

"Wait, Dawson," Diamond called after me, as I followed Bruno out to the parking lot. Trip followed and several other

8

pilots came after him, thankfully. The numbers seemed to be pretty even, though I didn't want to start a brawl.

"You guys stay out of this," I said to my friends. "Bruno and I are just gonna have a little talk, right Bruno?"

I didn't so much as turn to face him when his fist pounded into my cheekbone. Catching me off guard, I lost my balance, but quickly regained my composure and punched him back, easily breaking his nose.

One last fist to my face involved a glass bottle and large laceration near my eye.

"Back the fuck off," Trip said, getting in between us. The blood gushed, as head wounds generally did, and Trip got me back to my feet. The others held off the rest of the fight, and as Trip dragged me to his car, with the very shirt off his back held to my face, I could hear Bruno in the distance.

"You'll pay for this, pretty boy!"

"I don't know which way you need to lean your head, so just keep this pressed to your face and sit still," Trip instructed, as he sat me down in his front seat. I could hear Everett behind him bringing my luggage, which they tossed in the back.

"How bad is it?" Everett asked, already worried about my face.

"Probably gonna need a stitch," Trip said. "Gonna take him to the ER to get checked out just in case."

"I'll be fine," I said, through the closed car window.

"You know I have wedding crap to do, but keep me posted," Everett told Trip.

"How does your face feel?" Trip said, as he put the car in gear and sped off to the hospital.

"As you can imagine," I smarted off.

"Did he cut your eye?" Trip asked the magic question that could change the course of my future.

"Nah, I'm sure it's just swollen from the blow and my cheek got cut. I'll be fine."

Unfortunately, I wasn't sure if I was convincing him or me...

CHAPTER THREE

"You've got to be kidding me..." I picked up my ringing cell, and already knew the fate of my Lean Cuisine that was still cooking in the microwave.

"O'Neale," I said curtly, and listened for a second. "It's okay Selma, I'll be back as quick as I can. Give me about fifteen minutes."

Two heaping bites of rigatoni, and I tossed the rest in the trash, before grabbing my bag and keys and heading back to the hospital. *How many minutes did that frozen meal take?* Probably about four. So I had been home for five minutes, before getting called in again. I knew Selma was aware of how tired I was, and wouldn't have called if it hadn't been an emergency, but I also knew this was my life.

The life of an on-call emergency ophthalmologist wasn't nearly as grand as it sounded.

Once I got back in my Tahoe, I dialed the nurse's desk and hit send.

"Alright, Selma, I'm on my way, can you patch me to the nurse working the patient-in-distress, so I can get up to speed?" She was worried about me and I assured her, as always, I was driving hands free.

"Hi, Dr. O'Neale, this is Kaleb Wiseman, I'm taking care of your patient this evening," he explained.

"Hi, Kaleb, I thought you were working in the ICU tonight?"

"I was, but the E.R. is overrun, like usual, and needed some extra help, so I'm pulling a double. The patient-in-question has come in from a bar fight. From my assessment, he's taken a good punch to the cheekbone and will definitely need a stitch or two once we get the swelling down a bit... his eye is definitely bloodshot and I can't tell if it has sustained a laceration or what, but I felt like it was best to call you."

"Better to take precautions and check it out, I agree with you. Work on that swelling on his cheek with a cold compress, and I'll see you in about ten minutes," I told Kaleb, and hung up using the buttons on my steering wheel.

The hospital had a coffee shop that was thankfully open twenty-four hours, and conveniently, I had my favorite barista programmed in... she knew my order at this time of night.

"Doc O'Neale," Kisha called, as I zoomed through the front of the hospital, grabbing my double-shot latte with a pump of toffee-nut syrup. A little sugar and caffeine would fill my need for a lacking supper, and fuel me up for a little while, at least. "I was hoping you'd go home and get some rest, but you must be in for a long night."

"You got that right... I'll pay for this on my app when I get on the elevator."

"My treat tonight, Doc," Kisha said, with a warm smile. The platinum blondie had several coffee-shop locations in town, and I thought she took the graveyard shifts at ours, because her other locations closed at night.

The parking garage at the hospital was on the lower level, so I had a quick ride to the E.R. floor, and I'd be back in the thick of it. The elevator smelled like someone dropped a bottle of cleaning solution, which told me the night custodians were out and working. They did a good job of keeping things clean, but often got in my way, because they acted as though the hospital was closed. I powered my laptop back up in my arms as I exited the elevator. Kaleb was waiting for me at the nurses' station in the E.R.

"Evening, sir," I said to the young, good-looking nurse. Kaleb was in his prime, and it was mesmerizing to watch him work. I was pleased to hear he was assigned to me.

"Doc, lovely to see you again." His sarcasm was right on point, and I was quickly fiddling through the charts of a patient named Dawson Kaczmarek, before going in to examine him.

"Selma," I said. "Long time no see," I teased her, mostly because I knew she could take it, and we enjoyed the banter back and forth. She was in my corner for me working less and getting paid more, but together, we had ideas to solve that problem. I planned to approach my manager when the timing was right.

"Who's the attending tonight?" I asked, wondering if they were so busy Kaleb's observations were what I had to go on, or if someone had already seen the patient.

"It's Murdock tonight," Selma said, and rolled her eyes.

"He came in just as the patient was being triaged. Once he saw it wasn't an immediate issue, he left for another patient." Kaleb filled in the gaps. Murdock knew they'd call me back to take this patient off his list.

"Alright, Wiseman. Let's go see Mr. Kaczmarek," I said

and headed down to his bay. "We can update his physician from Murdock to me after I've examined him."

"Wait, how did you pronounce that?" he asked, catching me off guard.

"Kaczmarek. Kaa-ja-mar-eck," I repeated. "Why? Did he say it differently? Polish can have different inflections sometimes."

"No, he didn't say it at all and I stuck with Dawson, because I didn't want to butcher it. Man, you *can* do it all, can't you?" Kaleb elbowed me and made me smile.

"Phonetics isn't so bad," I told him.

I pulled the baby-blue curtain back to reveal a very nice-looking man splayed out on the hospital bed. A cold compress was on half his face, and the other half of his face did not seem pleased to see me. His friend, however, perked right up.

"Hi, there, I'm Dr. O'Neale. Mr. Kaczmarek?" I said directly to him, hoping he'd make eye contact. "How are you feeling, sir?"

"Heh, been better, but I'm okay... really... got in a little argument, and the other guy brought a piece of glass to the fight. Probably just need a stitch or two and I can be on my way."

"If I may, *Dawson*," the friend interrupted, giving him one heck of a look, and held out his hand to shake mine. I squeezed his hand tightly and waited for his explanation of *the look*. "Carter Clynes, Doctor. Dawson and I are both pilots. We have to pass rigorous sight tests in order to fly. I brought him just to make absolutely sure his sight has not been affected by this *little incident*."

"And you are wise to be such a good friend," I told him. Sitting my laptop down on the tray table, I grabbed a pair of gloves from the box on the wall and moved closer to

Dawson. I told him I was going to remove the compress to see what was going on underneath.

The cut to his cheek was nasty. And there was a chance he had a fractured cheekbone... an X-ray would tell us for sure.

"This is not going to be fun, but I'm going to hold your eyelid open for a few seconds so I can see what we're dealing with, okay?" Selma always praised my soothing voice with patients. I wanted them to feel safe in my hands, and I thought even the tough pilot was okay with that. He nodded. "Alright, hold still for me."

I lifted his eyelid and got a good look at what Kaleb described... bloodshot, was certain. And from first glance, he was on the verge of a detached retina, if not already.

The very idea that this man was a pilot and I was holding his career in my hands, hit me hard. In my profession, I'd seen injuries galore, of course, and many so much worse, but something about this particular patient drew me in. I felt his life spark, *his reason for being,* and couldn't handle the thought of it going away. I asked him a few questions and took a few notes.

"Gonna need an ultrasound, Mr. Kaczmarek," I said, and stepped away from him, while Kaleb put in the order and secured the machine.

"Ma'am, I hate to tell you this, but I was the one drinking tonight, not you. So, for you to think I might be pregnant is a bit of an overstatement."

A large chuckle came out, and I wished I had my cup of coffee that I left with Selma. I then realized he was serious.

"May I call you Dawson?" I said, and approached him again, so he could see me. The cold compress was back on his face and made it hard to turn his cheek.

"You may, ma'am," he replied. His friend, who I believed

said his name was Carter, was smirking as he leaned against the wall, observing our interaction.

"Dawson, dare I say... I *never* thought you were pregnant. One thing I learned in med school was that pregnancy typically doesn't happen to men... unless they are a species of seahorse. We actually can do an ultrasound on just about any part of the body. It's like taking a fantastic picture of the things we can't see from the surface."

"So I'm not pregnant?"

"Are you a seahorse?

"I don't think so?"

"I don't think so either, Dawson," I said, and patted his hand with mine.

CHAPTER FOUR

"Man? What are we doing here? Imma be fine!" I said to Carter, waiting for the doctor to *apparently* arrive back at the hospital. Who lets doctors leave anyway? "And where is this guy?"

"Dude, seriously. You have to get your eye checked out by a real eye doctor, and it's frigging late, of course she went home," Carter tried to explain, but the liquor was not helping my attention span. "You feel *fine,* because they gave you a local in your cheek, and your belly is full of liquor!"

He had a point.

But I still didn't like it.

My cheek felt cold with the compress on it, and that was the only sensation I could feel. The male nurse said they'd stitch it up once the doc gave the all clear.

"Wait, did you say *she* a second ago? My eye doc is a girl? How 'bout that." Nurse Kaleb was in and out of my bay and caught the tail end of that comment.

"She's an amazing doctor," Kaleb said. "Trust me, she's worth the wait."

I don't know whether Kaleb had a little crush on the ole

docky doc, or if she was just *that good*. Either way, I'd be sure to tease him after I met her.

I had my head laid back, while Trip leaned against the wall, absolutely refusing to sit down. I was at least a tidbit grateful for his company. Being a loner pilot often led to doing things by yourself, even when you didn't want to, so it was nice having him by my side.

The doctor came in while my head was laid back against the plastic pillow and I about gave myself whiplash when she came into the bay.

"Hi, there, I'm Dr. O'Neale. Mr. Kaczmarek?" Fuck me, she said my last name right. That *never* happened. I couldn't take my gaze away from her, but I also couldn't form many words. Trip was right about the liquor and the numbing shots on my face. I was indeed a tad loopy.

Her suggestion of an ultrasound was quite preposterous as well. Call it something else, why don't they?

And while I wasn't a seahorse, I declared I would have carried her babies.

"So what now?" I asked.

"Kaleb is getting the ultrasound machine as we speak, and you're going to lie back and take it easy. And while this is probably going to be hard for you, you mustn't move your head so forcefully or abruptly. I'm a little concerned about that eye, Dawson."

"Will you say it again?"

"The part about lying still?"

"No," I said, and turned ever so slightly, as instructed, so I could look into her eyes. "My last name."

"Ha!" she giggled, and her face was soon a full smile.

"Dawson Kaczmarek? Is that what you want to hear? Sir, I am very glad you are not in pain, but I think you might be a little tipsy," she said, and took hold of my hand to feel my pulse. We did not break eye contact.

Staring into her eyes was like looking into a sky of the Northern Lights. Greens and blues in different hues had me mesmerized. Did eye doctors take vital signs? Or did she want to just listen to my beating heart?

"You're one of the few to pronounce my last name correctly without having to be told," I explained. "It sounded nice hearing you say it."

Trip's eyes practically rolled out of his head, and the man *finally* sat down.

"I completely understand. People often look at my first name and then give me a double take, so I get it."

"What is your first name, if I may ask, Dr. O'Neale?" Was I being forward? Was this flirting? Or was this simply getting-to-know-you talk? Fucked if I cared. I was just ready to go. My eye was going to be fine. Who hadn't gotten in a bar fight once or twice before? I needed to know more about this lady.

"My first name is Vixie," she said, not taking time to look up from her slim laptop she was carrying around.

"Like Vixen?" *The reindeer* is what I wanted to say, but I refrained.

"Vixie... like my mother's name is Vickie and my father's name is Max, so they thought they'd be clever and put their names together to make mine."

Vixie.

Vixie.

It did have a nice feel on the tongue. I wanted to say it out loud again, but I didn't want her to think I was making fun of her name.

Kaleb came in with some weird machine, and then *Vixie*

told me to turn a certain way and lie very still. As long as I got to stare at her, I'd lie as still as she wanted.

"I think we're all set, Kaleb," she said, before popping my personal-space bubble. "I'll have some orders soon, and we'll work on getting Dawson fixed up." Fixed up? *With you, I hope!*

Trip was still engaged in our conversation and rolling his eyes every chance he got... not that I could see much of him with the sweet doctor leaning over me. But I certainly didn't mind...

CHAPTER FIVE

Oh, Dawson. You've done more damage than you realize. I'm gonna have to tell you surgery is in your future, and you're going to have to submit to my capable hands. But will you? Will you even take me seriously? You seem fun, but not so serious. I bet you're serious when you're flying. It's a sight I'd like to see myself one day. We'll get you back to your old self. You're just gonna have to trust me...

"Alrighty, that wasn't so bad, huh?" I said to him, putting the ultrasound machine back the way it arrived.

"Felt a little weird, but didn't hurt," he agreed.

"So, what's the verdict, Doc?" Carter interrupted our small talk.

"Well, boys, it could be a lot worse, that's for sure. Dawson, you do have what we refer to as a detached retina. And it will require surgery to correct it." *Was that tough to swallow?* I always tried to have the best bedside manner with patients.

"Whoa, surgery?" Dawson said, and tried to sit up. "This was just a little bar fight. Black eye, wham bam, thank you, ma'am. Surgery? You sure?"

"Hang on there, buddy. No sudden movements, remember? Keep that head of yours back on the pillow for me," I instructed him delicately. *Was I sure? Heh. Yeah, honey. I'm sure.* I needed more coffee if I was gonna have to explain myself. I instinctively guided his head back down, running my fingers through his dark hair, not wanting to let go once he settled. "All surgeries come with risks, but this is something we need to correct, and do soon, so it doesn't affect your vision moving forward."

"But will it, Doc?" Carter interjected. I appreciated his concern. Dawson certainly needed someone in his corner.

"It is possible. Some patients make full recoveries. Others have a little vision loss. We honestly won't know until the healing is complete," I told him. I realized I still had my hand on Dawson's forehead as I talked to Carter. And my other hand was resting on his chest, his hand over mine.

I helped patients all day long and never got such an electric current like I had with him. I had to pump the brakes and get my feelings in check. I needed some sleep, so I'd be ready for his surgery.

"Kaleb, see how quickly we can get an O.R. booked and ready. I'll be ready to scrub in first thing in the morning and have you prep Mr. Kaczmarek as soon as we can get on the schedule."

"Aye, ma'am," he said, making notes.

"Let's get Mr. Kaczmarek in line for an X-ray on this cheek too and stitched up." My instructions were clear. Kaleb and I had worked together many times, so he knew I meant business. The silent look he gave me told me he was concerned at the amount of hours I had worked straight through without sleeping. I didn't disagree with him either, but I wouldn't take the chance of leaving Dawson to someone else, whenever they might get around to scheduling him. That wasn't in me.

"I'll check and get right back to you, Dr. O'Neale," Kaleb said, and hurried to the front desk.

I should have followed him, but I stayed with Dawson a little while longer. My hand was still resting on his chest, he hadn't let go of me yet either, and I felt the concern he suddenly had once he realized surgery was going to happen.

"You're in good hands, ya know," I told him, and smiled. "I'm good at what I do."

Carter excused himself to make a phone call, and for a moment we were alone together in the small hospital bay. The light-blue curtain separated us from other patients, visitors and hospital staff, but for just a second it felt like he and I were the only two there. Why I had this sudden need to protect him, to care for him... the feelings were unusual for me.

"Am I..." Dawson sobered up for a moment and cleared his throat. "Am I... gonna lose my wings, Doc?"

"I'm going to do everything in my power to make sure you don't, Dawson," I squeezed his hand and said a little prayer in my head. I slowly pulled the compress off his head, as well as the gauze that Kaleb had packed in his cheek wound. He definitely needed a couple stitches, but with any luck, the scar would only be minimal if at all. "My friend, Dr. Rassmusen is working tonight, and he is excellent at facial wounds. I'm gonna see if he can take a look at this cut once you're out of X-ray, and see if he can't work a little magic, so you don't have too big of a scar."

"I hear dudes with scars get all the chicks," he said, and closed his eyes. Back to tipsy Dawson he went.

"I cannot confirm or deny that statement," I said, with a huge smile.

I'd take you with or without the scar.

Kaleb interrupted that thought, thank goodness. "We're ready to take him to X-ray," he said. "I've already got Dr. Rass from Plastics on standby for Dawson once he gets out of X-ray, and you give the okay after seeing his films... also, surgery is scheduled for 9 a.m." Kaleb gave me the look again, and I knew what it meant. I had about five hours to sleep before I'd need to scrub in once Dawson's X-ray came back.

He took the brakes off the bed, and I could see the nerves rise in Dawson, since Carter hadn't yet returned.

"I'll stay here and wait for your friend. I'm sure he won't be long, and neither will you." Dawson sighed, and gave a small smile. What he had going on was very routine, but for someone like him—a pilot—even minimal sight loss could mess up his career.

"You'll be here when I get back?" he asked, and Kaleb rolled his eyes. I couldn't help it when the patients took to me.

"Gonna grab a coffee and be right here waiting for you," I reassured him. Thankfully, he seemed to be my only patient for the moment.

CHAPTER SIX

The X-ray room felt like Elsa had prepared the table, and I immediately started shivering.

"It's always cold in here, man," Kaleb, the nurse, said. "Let me get you a blanket once we get settled."

He made sure I knew to stay still, that same broken record he and the Doc kept playing. What kind of mess had I gotten myself into?

"Was it a girl?" he said, as he brought a blanket over and covered me up.

"Was *what* a girl?"

"The bar fight. You do all this for a girl?" Obviously, I needed to sober up some more.

"Fuck," I sighed. "It was. And not even worth it. Chivalry is dumb sometimes."

Carter was right. I should have let it go.

"And you didn't even get to take her home! Man... that sucks!" Kaleb seemed like a cool guy. I wondered why he went into nursing, but didn't have the nerve to ask. "I just gotta say, if I was in your shoes, there's not another doctor

25

I'd want working on me. She's the best... you really *are* in good hands."

Kaleb's reassurance made me feel a little better, but I was still nervous as hell to have surgery on my eye. I kept hoping they'd look again and it would all be a big mistake. *It's just a black eye.*

Once I was covered up with some kind of weighted vest, Kaleb adjusted my head.

"K, you comfy? You're gonna lie right here super still and I'm gonna go into the booth," Kaleb said. "You'll be able to hear me talk to you in just a sec."

The X-ray took no time at all, and we were out of there and wheeling back to my bay in the emergency room, before I even had a minute to warm up. Carter was there waiting with Dr. O'Neale, just like she said. She was holding a large coffee too, and I suddenly felt bad she had been called in for me in the middle of the night.

"We will have films shortly, Doc," Kaleb said, and got my bed settled and locked back into position. "I'll head back and wait on them for you."

"How are ya feeling, Dawson?" Doc O'Neale asked, as she came over to the side of my bed with Trip.

"Trip, you get ahold of Kendall?" I asked, a little worried she might be concerned with us being out so late. He didn't want to text her until we knew what was up.

"*Trip*? You're a pilot and they call you Trip?" She was seemingly interested and I liked the bout of normal conversation.

"Yes, Dawson here has a nickname as well, but I'll let him save that embarrassment for another day," Trip said, and smirked at me.

"Yeah, yeah, another day..."

"So what airline do you guys fly? Are you local to Boca?"

She took a sip of her coffee, holding with both hands as if it was providing warmth. I suddenly wanted to hold her hands and warm them in mine. And ironically, I also wanted a coffee. Or some waffles. Or a turkey sandwich. Damn, I was hungry.

"I fly American Airlines. Trip here sold out and went private a while back, but that's where we met, *forever* ago."

"Y'all say I sold out. I sold up, good buddy. Simple schedules, much better money, home with my wife all the time, heh, sold out." Trip was right. He had a good life, one I could envy if I had a wife to come home to, but that wasn't for me. I enjoyed the thrill of never knowing where I'd lay my head, or who I'd lie down with. Which reminded me of what Kaleb had said earlier... after all this, it *was* too bad I didn't get the girl. *Or was it?* By the end of the fight I wasn't so pleased with Diamond.

Kaleb came in during our small talk and handed the doc some kind of folder with X-ray films. She excused herself to go look at them, I assumed.

"I talked to Kendall, and I'm gonna run home and change really quick and then come right back, so I'll be here for the long haul," Trip said.

"Man, you are not here to babysit me. You can go home for the night, I'll be fine," I told him, but the truth was, I wouldn't have minded him being in my corner. He was the only real friend I had in Boca.

"Nope, wife's orders are not to leave your side, other than to change out of these beer-stained clothes from the little encounter we had that got us here," he said. Trip was a good teaser, and it was a good thing he was wearing an undershirt, since he took his shirt off to stop my face from bleeding. "I brought your suitcase in, because I figured that was just the easy thing to do. You may not need clothes yet, but I figured you'd need a charger once they admit you."

"Admit me? Like I'm actually getting admitted to the hospital?" I asked him, remembering not to turn my head too swiftly as per instructions from pretty much the whole world. "I thought this was like an outpatient surgery?" *Fuck.*

"Hey man, it's all good. It *is* an outpatient surgery, but they're going to admit you so that you can stay here overnight, get fluids to get all this alcohol out of your system, and get your face taken care of before tomorrow morning." He was reassuring, but I still didn't like the idea. Trip hung around until the doc came back with at least a little good news.

"Cheekbone is A-OK!" she said, and smiled really big. Her teeth were so white and straight, her face practically lit up when she cheesed so big. "So, let's go over what's gonna happen next, so *Trip* can head home for a little bit and we can get you settled?"

When she looked over at Trip and said his name, it made me snarl a bit. I didn't like her saying his name and looking at him all friendly. *What the hell was wrong with me?* My emotions were out of whack and I needed to get a grip.

"Kaleb is working on getting you admitted," she said, and came over to stand beside me. I appreciated that she wanted to look in my eyes, and she knew that *I knew* that I wasn't supposed to move my head much. "It'll be easier for all of us if you're admitted just for tonight, since we have a few more things to do."

I still didn't like it, but it sounded better coming from her lips.

"Dr. Rass will be here soon to work on that cheek of yours now that we know nothing is broken." I liked looking into her eyes when she talked too. "At the same time, we'll get you hooked up to an IV to get you pumped full of fluids, and get that blood alcohol level down, so we can do surgery in the morning."

"Guess that means pancakes are out of the question?" I mean, I had to ask.

"Once you have tasted flight, you will forever walk the earth with your eyes turned skyward, for there you have been, and there you will always long to return."

-Leonardo da Vinci

CHAPTER SEVEN

Did he seriously just ask for pancakes?

"I tell you what, when we get this surgery over, we'll all have some pancakes."

"He'll hold you to that, Doc," Trip said. "The man loves pancakes."

Dawson's big grin assured me that Trip wasn't kidding either.

It was after 2 a.m., and my body was tired. The physical toll it took on a person working shift after shift was seldom appreciated. It was technically my day off, and another doctor, Simon Lenoir, was on the schedule starting at eight. Like hell I was letting Simon near Dawson though. He was old and grumbly and had no bedside manner. He seemed to be a fine ophthalmologist, but his rapport with patients, and well, everybody, was seriously lacking.

"I've got a couple things to finish up, and I'll come back and check on you when you get in your room. It'll give me a chance to explain how the procedure will go when I know you're a little more... sober..." I could hardly say it with a straight face. Dawson was cute when he was inebriated. And

31

the puppy-dog eye he gave me when I said I was leaving made me want to stay. I didn't get attached to patients like this either.

Dr. Rass arrived, and I shook his hand before introducing him to Dawson.

"Nice to meet you, Mr. Kaczmarek," he said, and I shook his hand too.

"He said it right too!" Kaleb hissed from the other room.

"Kaa-ja-mar-eck, Kaleb. Kaa... ja... mar... eck. You'll get it," Dawson said, and gave him a thumbs up.

I had already excused myself, but for some reason I kept lingering, and so did Trip.

"Trip, let me walk you out as I head up to the nurses' station?" He nodded and Dawson gave an okay for him to go. He had left Dawson's suitcase right beside the bed in case he needed it. Not many people came to the hospital already packed, unless they were having a baby, and we had already ruled that out, but it made sense a pilot would.

"He's gonna be just fine," I reassured him. He was handsome, so was Dawson. It was easy to see how the ladies would be all over them. And I thought it was good of Trip for getting out of that life and settling down. I was a little envious myself.

"I worry about him. He's reckless sometimes. The life of a playboy pilot isn't always easy," he told me. "I won't be but an hour or so. Need to get out of these clothes and get my phone charger."

A playboy pilot. Heh. That summed it up for sure.

"Take your time, Trip. These hospital chairs aren't comfortable in the slightest and that'll be your future for a while." He waved as he left the E.R., and after checking with Selma and telling her I was taking a break to sleep, I swung by Dawson's bay one more time.

Dr. Rass was about ready to fix up his cheek and administer a few small local shots to numb the area. This might not have been the best time for Trip to leave, not that I could see him rushing over to hold Dawson's hand, but it was kind of scary getting shots in general, much less in your face.

Dawson saw me standing in the opening of the curtain and waved his hand for me to come to his side.

"Can't move my head fast, ya know," he said.

"That's right. I see Kaleb got your IV in okay." I noticed he only had one stick, so that was good. Kaleb was one of the better nurses we had when it came to IVs.

"Not too bad at all."

"Dr. Rass is gonna numb your face so this is easier on you," I told him. Dawson reached out and took hold of my hand, not saying anything nor admitting he was anxious, just needing a little comfort. I could stand there and hold his hand. It was the least I could do. It seemed as though the poor guy didn't have any family in town, and we all knew he had already wrapped me around his little finger.

Literally.

His hands were cold. As most were in the hospital. The temperature was always chillier than you'd want it to be all year round and blankets were plentiful.

We had a bandage covering his injured eye, so he wouldn't be tempted to open it, especially while Dr. Rass was working on his cheek. Once he held tight to my hand, he closed his other eye and squeezed my fingers. Dr. Rass had started the local injections to numb the area, so he could easily glue it back together. He had a needle ready too as I assumed he was also needing to stitch an area of the cut as well. It was a nasty laceration, sort of looked like a lightning bolt, but Dawson was not just *a boy who lived*, he was a man, who I hoped would thrive when this was all said and done, and maybe at that point, we could be friends. I definitely wanted to get to know him better.

I didn't let go and stood there for the few minutes it took Dr. Rass, instinctively, *motherly* perhaps was the better word... *friendly*... *more than* friendly, I rested my other hand on his shoulder, wishing to offer some comfort, I guessed, I wanted to let him know someone was in his corner. I hoped he felt some relief with me being there. Truth was, I was a little nervous for him too. It's not like being in the hospital for any reason was *fun*.

"All done," Dr. Rass said, "I hope that wasn't too bad, Mr. Kaczmarek?"

Dawson opened his unbandaged eye, but still held tight to my hand. "Definitely been through worse, sir. Thank you."

Rass headed out and Kaleb came over to help finish cleaning up and bandaging Dawson's face.

"So uh, whatever that liquid was he was using on my face has, like run all down my back," Dawson said, trying to lie still. The saline Dr. Rass had used to clean the wound must have spilled. "And I know this shirt has blood all over it. Any chance you can help me remedy that?"

He looked up at me, but I knew he meant Kaleb, and thankfully Kaleb chimed in.

"These docs are always messy, man. I'll clean you up, no worries."

"Hey!" I snorted. "I'm not messy!"

"Oh, not you Doc, you're not messy," Kaleb said, and I could barely see him wink at Dawson, which made me smile. He was so good with patients.

I stepped back, so he could help him change, and as much as I wanted to see Dawson without a shirt on, it felt like a good time to excuse myself.

"Kaleb, I ordered a banana bag for our patient here, if you'd hook that up on a four-hour drip, I'd appreciate it. I'm gonna go check on the on-call room and see if it's full," I said. He nodded, knowing I needed to rest. "I'll see you soon, Dawson."

Sigh. I needed some sweet dreams...

"There's only one job in this world that gives you an office in the sky; and that is pilot."

— Mohith Agadi

CHAPTER EIGHT

"Is Dr. O'Neale hot?" I asked Kaleb when she left the room. "Like is this the alcohol talking, because my judgment is a bit confused this evening."

"Ha! Yes, she's hot!" His response was pretty immediate, so I wondered if *he* had a thing for the good doctor. "She's one of my favorites too. Course you already know that."

"You gotta a thing for her?" Hell, why not just ask.

"Even if I did, it wouldn't be worth risking our jobs... same goes for you... if you have a thing for her, best wait 'til you're healed up, and then pursue it. She can't date her patients."

"Oh I wasn't—" he cut me off.

"Just saying, man. That's all."

"She say something about a banana? Fuck, I'm hungry." I was still thinking about pancakes too.

"Oh, I wish it was a real bag of bananas for you. It's a bag of IV fluids... yellow like a banana... it'll get some electrolytes in you quicker, so you're ready for surgery in the morning. Helps with dehydration too."

I audibly sighed. Aggravated. Hungry. And, especially thirsty.

"Aren't hospitals famous for ice chips? Like, could that be a thing?"

"Let me check... I'm pretty sure you're technically NPO, but I doubt O'Neale would fight us over ice chips," he said, and went to look at something on his laptop.

"Ah, looks like you got your room assignment too. 323. There will be someone down here from transport to take you upstairs in a little bit." And I was just getting used to Kaleb too.

"Man, that's kind of a shame. I like you," I confessed.

"Right? That's how it goes. I'll swing by and check on you before I leave at seven," he said. "I'll grab you some ice to take upstairs too."

Kaleb's ice chips were wonderful. As if he had made them himself, I gave him all the credit. He hooked up the banana bag thing he promised, and shortly thereafter I was rolled up to 323.

After Trip left, I sent him a quick text and told him not to come back until the surgery. No need for him to just sit with me while I waited. With any luck, I'd catch a few zzz's before surgery.

I still couldn't believe I had fucked up this badly.

"Hi, honey, I'm Nurse Cocker. You'll have me until shift change." The nice lady took my vitals and helped me situate my pillow, instructing me not to move my head too much, and keep the head of the bed raised a bit so I wasn't lying flat. *Yeah. I know.*

"Dr. O'Neale says you're not going to be any trouble for me tonight, is she right?" she asked.

"You talked to Dr. O'Neale?"

"Yep, just a moment ago. She's at the nurses' station," she said.

"Oh, I thought she was going to be gone for a while, and no, ma'am, I'm not gonna be any trouble. I've had enough of that already this evening. All troubled out." I wanted to turn my head, get a glimpse at the door. See if maybe she was walking by. She was supposed to be going to sleep for a while before surgery, but she was up here. On *my* floor. Checking on *me*.

"Alright sweetie, I'm going to let you get some rest. I won't bother you unless you need me," she said, and showed me how to work the remote on the bed. I turned on the TV and flipped through the six stations, before reaching up to turn off the light.

I tugged the string and all the lights in the room came on. So I did it again and half went off. Again and the other half came on and switched some different lights on.

Then I dropped the string.

Whatever. Wouldn't be the first time I'd slept with the lights on. I was *not* going to push the nurse button.

"Are we having a rave in here?" Dr. O'Neale stuck her head in the half-opened door. The light from the hallway was even brighter when she came in. I winced a little as she closed the door behind her.

"Couldn't figure the lights out," I said. "Apparently, I'm having a rough day."

I was definitely sobering up, and still starving.

"Let me see what I can do," she said, and came over and turned the lights off. She left one very dim light on, so we could still see each other. "That better?"

"Much better, thank you." I wanted to reach out to her. Something about her presence was comfortable, but it wasn't in my nature to be vulnerable, especially not while sober. "I didn't think I'd be seeing you anymore tonight."

"Ah well, the on-call room was full, and it doesn't make much sense for me to go home, then turn around and come right back."

I felt bad. She was tired and I was keeping her from sleep.

"I thought I'd check on you and tell you about the procedure, if you're up for it?"

"Oh I'm definitely sobering up, no doubt about that. Also still hungry, but Kaleb managed to get me some ice chips. Hope that's okay."

"Yeah, ice chips are fine, just can't do any food this close to anesthesia. I'm sorry about that," she said, and walked around the hospital bed.

She sat down in the avocado-colored recliner next to my bed, but I couldn't turn my head to see her.

"Oh, I'm sorry, I'll get up. I can't stand it when I can't see someone talking to me, I won't do that to you," she said, and leaned against the bed, so I wouldn't have to turn.

"You're very good at this bedside manner thing," I told her, noticing a hair fall out of her messy bun atop her head and down into her eyes. I wanted to tuck it behind her ear, but I wouldn't cross that line. She tucked it herself and let out a big yawn. "I'm sorry I'm keeping you. I know you're tired. You had already finished your shift, and had to come back in for me, hadn't you?"

"Ah, don't you worry. This is nothing new for me." She winked at me. I patted the side of the bed and scooted over. "At least sit down while you tell me all sorts of things I'm not gonna understand." I shrugged my shoulders and enjoyed her smile. She complied though and sat down beside me, telling me about the surgery and the anesthesia—what would happen, and what I'd have to do after the surgery was over.

"Guess I'll be taking a little sabbatical," I said, still pissed at myself for getting into the fight in the first place.

"Fingers crossed, only a couple weeks. I've seen patients fully recover in that short period of time." I appreciated her optimism, and reached up to run my fingers through my hair, forgetting the bandage was tied around my head.

"Easy now, you forget you're a bit of a mess," she said, and adjusted the gauze so it would lie flat again.

"Yes, believe it or not, I'm usually *not* this much of a mess. I'm usually pretty smooth..."

"That's the thing about flying:
You could talk to someone for hours
and never even know his name,
share your deepest secrets and
then never see them again."

- *Jennifer E. Smith,*
The Statistical Probability of Love at First Sight

CHAPTER NINE

Smooth. *Yeah, he was smooth.*

It wasn't the first time I had sat on a patient's bed. It was just the first time I didn't want to get up. I fixed his hair and smoothed his bandages out.

My weight on the mattress made the plastic crinkle, and every time I heard that noise, I wished my patients were at home in their own comfortable beds, instead of in the hospital.

"May I make a suggestion?" I asked, and he nodded, of course, eager for my doctor-knowledge. "These hospital gowns are awful and the ties on the back are super uncomfortable to lie on. Since you don't have to worry about anyone seeing your backside, like some patients, we can untie these and then you won't have to lie on the strings."

"I like the way you think," he said. Kaleb had helped him change into some Jockey pajama pants and I knew why he'd suggested the hospital gown on top. It was hella easier, just not nearly as comfy as one's own pajamas.

I pushed the button on his bed and raised him up a little more, holding his neck in my arms, so I could untie the two

43

strings on his back. The top was easy to get to. The bottom one was a little tougher and I didn't want to jostle his head any more than necessary. Putting my arms around him felt nice. Like he would be someone I'd embrace on a normal day.

"And *you* get a little hug in the process," I teased him, holding him to my chest as I reached behind him.

"Don't mind if I do." His endearment was sincere.

The dim lights provided me a glimpse of his tanned back, a tattoo stretched across his shoulder blades, and I wanted to get a better look at it. *Another time maybe.* Once settled, I tucked him back in and told myself I needed to go. I was getting too attached to this one.

"Trip coming back to stay with you tonight?" I figured he'd have been back already.

"Naw, I told him just to get some rest and come back in the morning. Not like he's gonna sit here and hold my hand while we watch overnight Andy Griffith reruns."

I couldn't help but chuckle at the thought of the sight of the two of them doing that.

"Well, he's not!" I think it tickled Dawson too. "Hey... that bed over there? What are the chances of me getting a room-mate tonight?"

"Pretty slim, why? You rather be by the window?" It was the middle of the night, but I'd help him move if that's what he wanted.

"I was thinking you could take a little nap, actually. I know you're exhausted. There's an empty bed right here, and it seems as if you've been searching for one." Man, was that tempting? There were several openings on Dawson's floor, and I had actually planned to find an empty room to sleep in, since the on-call room was full.

"I mean, I'm sure that'd be frowned upon... you're my patient after all."

"Who am I gonna tell?" he asked. And truth be told, nobody would have cared, other than Dawson. Gretchen, his nurse, was fifteen years my senior, and had already told me to go find somewhere to sleep.

I pulled the curtain back to the wall so the room was no longer separated.

"How about an episode of Andy Griffith and I'll sit over here and close my eyes for a few minutes?"

"Sounds good to me," he said, and turned the TV channel. "I sure don't mind the company."

"Want me to scoot your ice chips closer before I lie down?" It was the least I could do.

"It's like you can hear my stomach growling!" I could actually hear his stomach growling every once in a while.

"I meant it when I said we'd all have pancakes when surgery is over... I'll make good on that promise." I liked Dawson and his friend Trip. Surprisingly, the hospital cafeteria actually had fantastic breakfast options.

Including blueberry pancakes.

I sat down on the empty bed and slid my shoes off. I had already clocked out, so I didn't feel bad about taking a break for a few.

The familiar whistle of the Andy Griffith theme song and a glance over at Dawson was all I needed. Just being in the same room with him felt good.

I was going to be sad when it was time for him to be discharged.

"Flying starts from the ground.
The more grounded you are,
    the higher you fly."

                    - J.R. Rim

CHAPTER TEN

It wasn't but a few minutes into the black and white TV show, and Doc O'Neale was out. Her tiny snores were more like kitten purrs, and I enjoyed the fact that I wasn't spending the night in the hospital alone.

Truth was, it *was a little scary*.

I had spent the better part of a decade on my own, fending for myself and doing just fine. In high school, I started learning how to fly through a local tech prep program, where I got to learn by doing crop dusting. I already had some hours under my belt, which helped in college.

I was in a mountain of debt by the time I finished my degree and certifications to get my license.

I was thankful my parents were able to see me graduate, because my mom passed away shortly thereafter. My dad pushed me to go on with my life, knowing my profession didn't leave much time for family, but I did as he wished, and kept on.

A couple years later, he was diagnosed with Huntington's Disease... we all knew his memory was never good and just hoped it worsening was not in his future. We didn't always get what we wished for. After a few years of flying and working a ton of overtime, I had paid down my student loans, and began paying the bills at the retirement center for my father. His own savings was depleting fast at the time and I felt like it was the least I could do.

But hard times like these, sitting in a hospital bed with no real family, sure made me miss my mom. I gathered that Dr. O'Neale was a couple years younger than me and her presence was nice. It was nice having someone in my corner.

Kendall, Trip's wife, would baby me when she came to the hospital the next day. She always took great care of me when I was a guest in their home. I think she knew that she and Trip were often the family I didn't have.

Andy Griffith just so happened to be my dad's favorite TV show. At some point, in the midst of Otis checking himself into the jail and the doc's sweet snores, I too drifted off to sleep.

The incessant beeping woke me from a sound sleep, and Gretchen, errrr, Nurse Cocker, was fiddling with the IV machine. The bed beside me was empty and had been remade. She'd left while I was asleep.

"What's the verdict, Nurse Cocker? Are we done banana-ing?"

She chuckled. I thought about how it must be hard working nightshifts, constantly in and out of rooms while patients were trying to rest.

"You are officially done banana-ing. I have to hook up a regular saline drip for a little bit, and you'll be done with this thing before your procedure..." she paused. "Now, I can imagine you need some help getting to the restroom?"

"I thought you'd never ask." *Hell, yeah,* I had to pee. She was certainly right about that.

"Let's take it slow and I'll help you with the IV cords." Nurse Cocker had obviously done this a time or two. When I got up out of the bed, the back of my hospital gown fell open. Thank goodness for my pajama pants, or she'd have had that nice view of my backside, like the doc had mentioned.

"Oh, you've come untied. No worries, sweetie. I'll help you get put back together when you're all finished."

It was weird walking around with an eye patch. My depth perception was most certainly off, and boy, did I have a headache. I quickly took care of business, and declined the jolly nurse's offer to help me tie back up and just lay back down on the bed. Doc was right, it was much more comfortable that way.

And just as I had a chance to look at my phone to see what time it was, in came Trip and Kendall.

"Dawx! Sweetheart, what have you done to yourself?" Kendall came in arms open wide, ready to mother me. She really was a saint and I appreciated that she cared. Trip sat down in the recliner and Nurse Cocker excused herself. It was a little over an hour before the procedure, so I figured things would get rolling pretty soon. Kendall sat on the edge of the bed when she finally stopped hugging me.

"You gave us quite a scare!" she said. "If we'd have had someone to watch Brucey last night, I'd have been up here too."

"I know, and I love you guys... I did okay last night," I said. *I had a little company...*

"I am flying blindly but sure to meet some day...wait for me!"

- Archana Singh

CHAPTER ELEVEN

Seeing that girl embrace Dawson the way that she did, and then sit down on the bed beside just as I had the night before, made a rage rise in me I had never felt before.

Get it together, Vixie. You're his freaking doctor.

I took a deep breath, standing at the threshold of his room, watching them interact, before knocking and opening the door all the way.

Knock, knock.

"Sorry to interrupt, how's my patient this morning?"

"Hey, Doc, doing okay," he said, smiling at me. Kendall stood as if she had been caught by the school teacher, and gave me space to walk around the bed to check on Dawson.

"Hi, there, I don't think we've met?" I said to her, noticing Trip had returned and was sitting in the recliner.

"Dr. O'Neale, this is my wife, Kendall," he said, and stood up.

"Nice to meet you. Trip says you are the best, and we couldn't be happier to have you taking care of one of our dearest friends." *Okay, maybe she's not that bad.* And she was married to Trip, so... I figured I'd excuse her.

I turned my attention back to Dawson.

"I'm glad you got some rest," he said. The smile on this man made my knees weak.

"Me too. I have an important procedure this morning," I teased. "I'm glad you got some rest too."

I checked out his IVs and he'd had enough fluids prior to the procedure. Most of these surgeries were outpatient, and I explained that to Dawson, but given the nature of his hospital entrance, it made more sense to admit him. So once surgery was over, he'd be in recovery for a little, and then come back to his room where he'd hopefully be discharged fairly quickly afterward.

"Guys, if you wouldn't mind stepping out for just a minute, while I talk with Mr. Kaczmarek?" Kendall and Trip quickly exited, which made me feel more at ease with Dawson.

"How long did you stay with me last night?" he asked. "You're freshly showered and have on a new doctor outfit."

Damn, he was cute. A new doctor outfit.

"Ha. Yes. I stayed a couple hours and got a nice nap in. Thank you for the invitation."

I *had* to keep it professional.

"Ready to do this?" I asked.

"Nervous, but ready. I feel like a pirate with this eye patch, and way off my game."

"Let's go ahead and take this bandage off Dr. Rass put on last night," I told him. "And let me get a good look at that eye this morning before we head downstairs."

No surgery was ever routine, as people often referred to procedures. Knowing someone's sight was in my hands, always came with pressure and responsibility, and even more so with Dawson for some reason. What we were dealing with was textbook, I was thankful for that, not because I couldn't handle a challenge, but because I wanted him to heal and get back to living life as quickly as possible.

"You remember what you promised me, right?" he asked, as I finished my quick exam, and put the eye patch back over his eye.

"Yep, I'm gonna take great care of you... you're in good hands."

"Well, that, yes. But the other promise..."

I started to wonder what I'd said while I was exhausted at 3 a.m., as it dawned on me.

"Pancakes."

"Ding, ding, ding!" he practically cheered. "I'm still hungry!"

"Ha, pancakes are on the menu once you're good to go post-op."

"Deal."

"Anything you want to discuss before your friends come back in? I always like to ask my patients while we are alone, just in case." You never knew when someone had a question or concern they did not want to bring up in front of a family member.

"I'm not gonna lie, I'm nervous, but you already know that. I've got my game face on, and I'm ready to roll."

I reached over and squeezed his hand. "It's shift change for the nurses, so someone new will be in shortly... and we're on schedule for surgery, so as soon as transport gets here, I'll meet you downstairs, okay?"

"It's a date."

I told Trip and Kendall they could go back in, and I hovered around the door to his room a little longer than I probably should have. I overheard Kendall hugging and kissing Dawson and telling him she had to go help with some kind of wedding stuff, but Trip would be staying for

53

the duration of the procedure, and be here for Dawson when he got out. That made me feel better.

It was time to scrub in and I needed to get my own head in the game. I had worked way too much over the past week and it was catching up to me. Dawson's surgery was the only thing on my schedule and I planned to relax when it was all said and done.

When they wheeled him in to me, he had stripped out of his hospital gown and was covered in a sheet above the waist. His feet and pajamas sticking out at the end of the bed.

"Kendall spilled my ice chips on my lovely nightgown. Oh, and they had melted, so it was a nice cold cup of water all over me," he said.

"Nurse didn't get you another gown?" I tried not to laugh.

"I didn't ask. They suck anyway. This sheet okay? Back to my comfortable T-shirt for me when we're done here."

I introduced Dawson to the small team of helpers that I had, and we got down to business.

"I'm going to put a clear bandage over your cheek so your cut stays nice and clean during the procedure. We'll remove it later, okay?"

"You're the boss. So, I start counting backwards or something?"

He was so cute, I couldn't help but laugh at him.

"See ya on the flip side, Dawson."

"See you in my dreams."

I made sure to get a good look at what I'd missed during Kaleb's shirt change the night before. The man had abs I could have sat and watched all day.

The poor thing needed some *pancakes*.

CHAPTER TWELVE

The sight of Dr. O'Neale at the head of the bed I was lying in as it lowered down into her lap for the procedure was just heavenly. The lights above her head made it appear she was wearing a halo and my angel to take care of me through the procedure.

I remembered hearing something about "the body of a G.I. Joe" and a "hunky pilot can fly my plane", but those voices were coming from around me, and not from Dr. O'Neale.

I rarely remembered dreams, but this induced sleep took me back to my early days as a pilot. The nerves, the worry. Making sure I crossed all the Ts and dotted all the Is. The check lists. The flight times. Flying in storms and flying at night. Making sure I got enough sleep to fly.

I wasn't in a deep enough sleep that I was completely out of it. I could hear bits and pieces of what was going on around me. Dreams paired with the voices clouded together, and I felt a bit like I was floating. The real reason I was in that chair, in the arms of Dr. O'Neale, was the furthest from my thoughts.

"Heeeey Dawx," Carter said, and seemed to be saying it over and over again. "Doc told me to talk to you as you were waking up... I know my voice is *sooooo* soothing. I should have made you a playlist instead."

"Rrrrr." A grunt was all I could manage.

"There he is, come on buddy."

"I. Am. Not. A puppy dog." Opening my good eye was strange. A different patch that felt much more official was now over my other eye. I remembered though that I'd have a patch for a day, until I came back in to have it removed.

It just occurred to me that my appointment would be on a Saturday. Did they do that kind of appointment on the weekend? And would Doc be available? I suddenly hated to drag her on an off day if she wasn't.

"Dawx, buddy. You're breathing kinda hard." Trip reached over and squeezed my shoulder, and it pulled me out of the dream gate I kept flirting with.

"Hmmm?" I opened my eye again, and this time, tried to move a little bit. "Man, those sleepy medicines are weird as fuck."

Trip laughed at me. Hell, I'd have laughed at me too. I was a sight.

I heard him tell a nurse I was waking up.

"How ya feeling, sweetcakes?" she came over and said to me. "Dr. O'Neale asked to be paged when you started to wake up, so she'll be here in just a few minutes."

"Sweetcakes... heh heh."

"He's gonna be a little loopy for a bit, but it sounds like he's coming out of the anesthesia just fine," she said to Trip. I could hear her talking like I wasn't there, but my eyelid was just so heavy, it did not want to stay open. I also was very distracted by the endearing *sweetcakes* that she had

called me. My stomach had not forgotten it was hungry—
for sweet *pancakes*.

Dr. O'Neale came in, and I promise you, I tried real hard
to open my eye and be a good, awake boy.

"Hey, Dawson," she said. Her voice was much more
soothing than Trip's.

"Hey, *sweetcakes*, he he he," I giggled, realizing after I
said it that using that term of endearment on my doctor
might not have been the most appropriate thing to say.

"Feelin' good?" she asked. I could see her smile when I
did get my eye open enough to pay attention to my
surroundings. "Yeah, this loopy feeling will wear off really
soon, and you'll be able to go back to your room."

"Am I still your favorite pirate?" *What? Where did that
come from? It seemed like the thing to ask at the time.*

"Oh yes, you most certainly are my favorite pirate."

"Pirates like to drink rum, and the rum you gave me was
much stronger than what I had last night. I might not have
even thought to punch Brutus if I had been enjoying this
particular beverage. Hey, Trip, was his name Bruuuutus?"

"Uh, I believe it was Bruno," he chimed in.

"Yeah. That's it. Bronson."

I reached over and took hold of Dr. O'Neale's hand. I
couldn't tell if anybody else saw me do that, because my eyes
were closed, but when I finally opened my good eye again, I
saw she was staring at me, and she looked happy holding
my hand.

"It's always nice when a patient has a good reaction to
anesthesia. Some do not." She said these words, I thought,
to Trip, but I was still pleased to hear I was having a good
reaction.

"So Doc, when do I get my pirate patch removed?"

"Likely tomorrow. We'll make you a follow-up appointment and take a look then. See if we can leave the patch off for good."

I took a deep breath and felt the drunkenness subside. Eye open, this time for good. I was now awake enough to actually focus.

"There he is," Trip said, at the end of the bed.

"So, give it to me straight, how'd it go?" Dr. O'Neale said all the things I expected her to say. And I was pleased to hear it went well and my recovery time was projected to go smoothly. "You kept your promise."

"Yep. One promise, at least." If I'd have even been able to, I'd have turned my head and questioned her. "I promised I'd take good care of you, and I also promised pancakes, which I still intend to deliver..."

"You're going to deliver pancakes?! Like a pizza?!" Trip's chuckle at my words reminded me I was still hung up on my "rum" and I realized what she meant. "Ah, well, pancake delivery *should* be a thing."

It was at that point I realized she was still holding tightly to my hand.

And loopy or not, I had no intentions of letting go.

CHAPTER THIRTEEN

My word, was he a cutie!

His little mannerisms as we talked just made me want to melt right there. At least I got through the surgery without ogling him. Being attracted to a patient really added a level of stress I was unprepared for... in fact, it made me reassess our doctor/patient relationship, and I had to cool it in my brain long enough to get through the surgery.

"Pancake delivery should totally be a thing," I agreed. Trip shook his head too. It wasn't a bad idea at all.

Pancake delivery. I was about to make that happen. It would be an easier way to fulfill my promise too. The staff took Dawson back up to his room, while I swung by the cafeteria and saw my favorite chef, who was thankfully working.

"This is a special request, and since it's technically brunch at the moment, I'm hoping you can do me a helluva favor," I asked. James had worked as a chef in the cafeteria the entire time I had been at Good Samaritan Hospital and was always willing to help out a patient with dietary needs or requests. Even the occasional staffer who was starving at an off hour as well.

"I'll take care of it, Doc!" he said, and tipped his chef hat.

"I'll go take care of the bill right now," I told him, but he wouldn't let me pay. We got a free meal if we worked a double, and I rarely took advantage of that perk. I was usually too busy, so he told me I had it coming and not to worry. James was a good man, and I appreciated him.

My coffee and early morning nap were wearing off, so I was glad that I was able to clock out once Dawson was discharged. While I had thoroughly enjoyed having him as a patient, my extra shifts were starting to catch up to me, and I realized just how tired I was.

A quick email to management while I was speed walking back to the third floor and I felt better. I had to do something about my schedule.

"How ya feeling Dawson? Anesthesia all worn off?" I asked, after a few minutes at the nurses' station and updating records.

"I'm feeling kinda like I have two hangovers, if I'm being honest?"

"Honest is good. You should always be honest with your doctor."

Trip snickered in the hospital room recliner.

"Takes a little time to get discharge paperwork processed," I said. "So, I ordered a little surprise for you to enjoy while you wait... if that's okay?"

"Doctor's orders? A surprise? Is this a good surprise?" Dawson seemed a little nervous at the sound of my suggestion.

"I hope it's a good surprise!" And right on-time, the lovely Felisha rolled in a cart from the cafeteria.

"Wait a minute," Dawson said, and turned his nose up like a bloodhound. "For a man who hasn't eaten in practically twenty-four hours, my sense of smell is hoping it's not being fooled."

"No sudden head movements, 'kay?" I reminded him. "And yes. You're smelling pancakes. And bacon. And all sorts of other things. Thank you, Felisha. And please thank Chef James for me again. I'll bring this cart back downstairs in an hour or so myself."

"Aye, Doc O'Neale! Have a good day, all!"

"Oh, the day has just gotten exponentially better," Dawson said.

"Chef James is a buddy of mine, so this should be pretty good," I said. "And not on the regular dietary menu." I put his tray in front of him and scooted the other bed's tray table over to Trip.

"Oh my goodness," he said, "For me too?"

"We're all having brunch this morning, boys. After last night, you've earned it."

I took the lids off, placing them on the bottom shelf of the cart, so I could be sure to return everything.

"He said he'd make you the *Chef James Special Spread*," I could hardly say it with a straight face, "...and I think he outdid himself!"

"Blueberry pancakes, chocolate chip pancakes and regular pancakes with fruit and maple syrup. Man, Doc, when you make a promise, you deliver," Dawson said.

"Eating is gonna be a little weird at first. Patients don't realize how much they move their head until they're supposed to keep still, so let that elbow of yours do the work," I suggested.

I noticed that Trip got up and fixed Dawson's coffee the way he liked it, which I thought was very telling of their friendship. He even added a pack of sugar to Dawson's orange juice, which made me laugh.

"It's the only way he'll drink it," Trip said. "I've known this guy a long time."

"We're not together as often as we'd like to be," Dawson said, "But we sure can pick up where we left off."

"Alright y'all this bromance of yours tells me Dawson is going to be in good hands... is he staying with you, Trip? Until he heals?"

"Well, that's one thing I was going to talk to him about. For sure tonight, Kendall wouldn't let him get away that soon. But, Dawson, I wondered if you'd want to stay at my old place at Silver Shores?"

I learned later that Trip stayed in touch with the folks at his old homestead, and his old condo was available to rent for the month. They didn't let in folks under fifty, but Trip had made a call and secured the place for Dawson to stay.

"Dude, I'm not old enough for Silver Shores," he said, and took a big bite of pancakes.

"Neither was I, but it sure worked out. We can talk about it later. I just want you to be as comfortable as possible."

"That's a really nice offer, Trip," I told him. I knew of Silver Shores from a few patients that lived there, and even though it was for residents much older than Dawson, it sounded like a fantastic place for him to be cared for as he healed.

CHAPTER FOURTEEN

"You made my day with the pancakes," I told Dr. O'Neale as we were finishing up. It was nice to have an adult conversation with her and Trip, and not be intoxicated and/or worried about my eye. "So, will I come back here tomorrow for my follow-up?"

"Well, that's something I was going to ask you... I can make you an appointment with the ophthalmologist that's on the schedule," she said, and paused, obviously seeing my reaction was not pleasing. "...or I can make a quick house call tomorrow and check on you myself. I don't normally offer to do that, but I'm not working tomorrow, and you're kind of a special case."

"Oh, he's a special case, alright," Trip said, interrupting and making Dr. O'Neale smile. I'd have encouraged him to say something else if I thought she'd grin again.

"That okay with you, man?" I asked. "After all, I'm in your care til I get settled at Silver Shores."

"Of course, if Dr. O'Neale doesn't mind the house call, that's perfectly fine with us."

"Don't mind at all," she said. "How about I give you my

personal cell, *as long as you don't tell anybody*, and you can text me the address tomorrow?"

"Works for me," I said, and handed her my phone, so she could put her number in. "If you call yourself when you get your number saved, you'll have my number too, so you know who I am when I text you later."

"Give us a little bit to get your discharge papers, and you'll be free to go, 'ay?"

I knew my eyes were playing tricks on me, but the way she stood there, she just had a glow about her. I couldn't even explain it to myself, but I was convinced it was the anesthesia and pain meds.

"Thanks again, Doc," Trip said, as she headed back out to the nurses' station.

Waiting a minute before he said anything, Trip stood at the head of my bed staring at me, while I was obviously in La La Land.

"What?"

"You tipsy from the meds, or are you crushing on your doctor?" Trip was blunt when it came to shit like that.

"Shut up, man. It's been a rough twenty-four hours."

They insisted on wheeling me out of the hospital in a wheelchair, despite my protests and promises that I could walk. Trip took my suitcase and Dr. O'Neale caught the elevator with us as we were leaving the floor.

"I'll take him for you, Charlotte. I'm heading home anyway," she said, and took hold of my wheelchair.

"Thank you, Dr. O! See you in a few days!" the Charlotte person said back.

"I told them I could walk," I said, noticing Trip trying to keep a straight face.

"You're not the first, Dawson. This is standard procedure.

We have to make sure you're good to go before you head out."

"Well I'm good. I promise." Was it pride? Was it embarrassment? Was it the fact that I didn't want a beautiful doctor pushing me around that bothered me?

"Trip, if you want to pull up in the drop-off circle, I'll wait here with Dawson," she said, and Trip nodded. *A few minutes alone.*

"I can't thank you enough for being so good to me. Somehow I don't feel like all patients get such special treatment," I said, as she applied the chair's brakes.

"They don't all get pancakes, that's for certain, but I try to be as compassionate as I can with each one, and take care of their whole body... and not just their eyes."

Oh fuck, I wanted her to take care of my whole body.

"How's the face pain? From the fight and the stitches?" she asked.

"Feels like I got in a fight?" I shrugged my shoulders.

"Sounds about right. When are you moving into Silver Shores?"

"Tomorrow afternoon, I think. Trip just needed to move some furniture around, and Kendall wanted me to stay at the house tonight. I'm sure she'll be ready to get rid of me by morning."

"How about I meet you there tomorrow then? Help you settle in a little?"

"I'd like that, I mean, if that's alright?"

"I rarely have plans on my days off anymore. I'm usually on call, so I typically just catch up on laundry. Trust me, it's alright." She waved when she saw Trip pull up and open the passenger door for me.

"Remember, no swift movements of that head of yours.

Rest. And take it easy, K?" she instructed. "You're in good hands, Dawson."

"He sure is, my hands are great," Trip said.

I tried to wink at her with my unbandaged eye and I realized how silly that must have looked.

"See ya, Doc."

"See ya, Dawson..."

CHAPTER FIFTEEN

What a fine specimen of a man...

Of course, my phone buzzed the second Trip's vehicle was out of sight. I was cursing in my head thinking I was getting called back in to work, when instead it was my mother. Not any better really. I knew she was calling to hound me.

"Hi, Mom, what's up?"

"Oh, honey, I wasn't expecting you to answer at this time of day. I was planning to leave you a message."

"Well, I did, so tell me live instead." I tried not to be smart with her, but every time she or my father called, it was about my job, or a blind date of some sort.

"I was hoping you'd be free for dinner tonight?" In most cases, when my parents asked me to come to dinner, it involved some sort of interrogation regarding what I was doing with my life. I was tired and approaching grouchy stage when she asked, and I was not in the least interested.

"I'm at the end of a long week and need to catch up on sleep, any chance Sunday would work instead?" Maybe putting her invitation off would sit better than a complete no?

"Sure, honey, you can come by on Sunday, but your cousin is in town tonight and I thought you might want to see him?" *You could have led with that, Mother.*

"Denny is in town?" I clarified. Denny and I were the same age and practically grew up together. If I wasn't at his house when we were kids, he was at mine. We were inseparable until high school, when we went off to different schools.

"Yep, he's in town for a conference, had a free night for dinner and called." *He didn't call me.* "Dinner is at six, if you want to come by."

"Alright, Ma. I'm running on fumes, so I need to go home and nap for a couple hours, but I'll be there."

"You can still come Sunday too... if you want," she added, before I hung up. I knew that was a mistake when I offered, especially before knowing the whole story.

I hopped in my Tahoe with visions of my fluffy pillow where I planned to lay my head.

It was time to rest.

When I pulled up into the half-circle of the building where my parents lived, I saw Denny standing outside smoking. After I left the nest and went to college, my parents decided they wanted a simpler life, with staff and a better view than what we had at my childhood home. So, they bought a penthouse of a swanky resort condominium and had fresh sheets on the daily, and lots of room for guests who wanted to take a trip to the beach.

"What? You call your aunt, but not your favorite cousin

when you're coming to town?" I couldn't hold back the hounding.

"You're just like me, busy. And I figured Aunt Vickie would know your schedule."

"And this habit? You haven't kicked it yet? You're a doctor for Christ's sake." I had no problem getting on his case.

"And your point? Doctors have vices too. And I only smoke one or two a day, max."

"Max is my father. Come give me a hug and I'll leave you alone." There was something about a hug from an old friend. We weren't just cousins. We'd had each other's back as long as we had been walking, and the familiarity was nice.

"Before we go up there," he said, letting go of the big squeeze he had around me. "You should know I brought a friend."

"You brought a friend for dinner? Thought you were here for a conference. Who is she? Tell me all the deets!" I was excited at the fact he had a girlfriend. Denny wasn't one to date often.

"Not exactly. A colleague from work. He's a cardiologist in my practice."

"Why the warning then?" I was stumped.

"Because he's good looking and I get the feeling Aunt Vickie is gonna try to play matchmaker."

"Fucking fantastic. I knew I should have stayed home." He laughed at my potty mouth.

"But then you wouldn't have gotten to see me!" Denny threw his arm around my neck and kissed my temple. "At least it'll be good food. If your doctor life is anything like mine, a decent meal is always welcome!"

"Well, you're not wrong there!"

"Hey, Mom. Dad." I said, when we got off the elevator to

the penthouse. When I walked inside, I could see a dark-haired gentleman out of the corner of my eye.

"Denny, I see you're back. Vix, let's go into the library, so Denny can introduce you to his colleague that he brought to dinner." My mother was quite the instructor when it came to who did what and when they did it.

"Sure, Mom," I said, and sat my purse on the bureau near the door.

"It's nice to see you in real clothes, sweetheart," she said, and kissed me on the cheek. "Scrubs are quite becoming, but I like seeing you still have a figure."

"Mom!" I hushed her, and Denny laughed. He sank down into the large sofa across from my father.

The doctor colleague was intrigued by my father's impressive collection of rare books and could barely look away.

"Vixie, meet my colleague, Dr. Zak McIntyre. Zak, this is my cousin, Dr. Vixie O'Neale."

"Nice to meet you," I said, and reached out my hand to shake his. When he walked a step into the light, I got the first full glimpse of a handsome face with perfect stubble and green eyes that immediately charmed me.

"Nice to meet you, too," he said back. Denny pulled me down on the couch next to him in an effort to bring me back to reality and shoo away the stars floating around my head. *Heck yeah, it was nice to meet you.*

CHAPTER SIXTEEN

"Kendall, honey. You know I love you *and* appreciate you, but you don't have to wait on me."

"Oh, Dawx, it's only for one night. You need to rest and it makes me feel good taking care of my boys... so keep that head elevated and don't strain your good eye!" She liked to be bossy sometimes too. Truth was, I appreciated that Trip and Kendall had gone out of their way to take care of me after the accident. They were the closest thing to family I had down in Florida.

I was set up in the recliner and resting as per my home nurse's instructions. She kept bringing me drinks and offering to make me snacks. Kendall had already started washing all my laundry, while Trip was over at Silver Shores making the arrangements for my impromptu *vacation*.

Good thing was I didn't need round-the-clock care. I think staying there was more to get me out of their hair, since I couldn't really play with Brucey, or hang out too much, at least until I healed. And they knew I'd be taken care of in the retirement community.

I was looking forward to the Doc's visit to remove the

bandage and give me further instructions on what I could and couldn't do, but for twenty-four hours, I could chill and take it easy.

Trip came home and we shot the shit for a spell, while Kendall made an amazing spaghetti supper. I could smell it the whole time we sat in the living room talking. And I'd thought the pancakes smelled good at the hospital.

Maybe I *was* a seahorse and pregnant. Pancakes and spaghetti seemed like something a pregnant woman would eat. I'd have to remember to tell the Doc that.

"So, tell me again how *you* snagged a beautiful woman, who is currently cooking *me* dinner?" Trip laughed at the sentiment.

"Just got lucky, man!"

Kendall called from the kitchen. "Dawx, do you want to try to sit at the table, or would you like me to bring a tray to you? I don't want you to overdo it."

"I'd like to try sitting at the table. I promise to be on my best sloth-inspired behavior."

"You're all setup at Silver Shores. We can check you in after 9 a.m. tomorrow. I just wanted to make sure your bed was ready."

"My bed was ready?" I questioned him, as I slowly sat up in the recliner. It was hard not moving at my normal pace and I had to pay attention. My inner truck needed a governor and I didn't like it one bit.

"Yeah, I asked them to put a bed in your room that could raise the head to make it easier for you to prop yourself up at night."

"A hospital bed? Really, Trip?"

"Doc O'Neale said this healing business was no joke. You're gonna have to follow orders to a T if you want your sight to come back." I knew he was right. I just didn't like it.

"A hospital bed just seems so... so *geriatric*." I couldn't help it. It did. And I was far from an old man.

"Don't you think I know that? Kendall has plans to make it more comfortable though. She was out shopping this morning for new sheets and a mattress pad." *They really were good friends*. "Let's go eat, I'm starving."

"Tell Brucey after I get better, we'll wrestle around and have some uncle time," I told Kendall, as she was tucking him in. I felt bad that I couldn't play with my buddy, but we all agreed our roughhousing would have to wait. "Thanks for dinner, too."

"We'll have some Tiramisu once I get little man settled," she said, and took off down the hallway to his bedroom. Trip and I discussed how things had changed for him since he had started flying for the private sector, and I was a little envious of his nights and weekends spent back at home with Kendall and Brucey.

"What's your long-term, man? When are you planning on settling down?" he asked.

Settling down? Eww. The thought was one I had many times, but never had any reason to pursue it. I wasn't the type to settle down. I had a huge future ahead of me and planned to continue traveling the world.

Well, hopefully. If my eyesight fully returned, that was the plan.

"When you get the all-clear, we'll go fly together. I wanna show you how the other side lives," Trip said.

"I will take you up on that."

I couldn't get the idea of settling down, or the face of a certain doctor out of my head the rest of the night.

73

"I'm packing up the rest of this tiramisu to take over to Silver Shores," Kendall said. "And I'll grab you some groceries and bring meals over too so you don't have to worry about it."

"I can order delivery too. I may not be able to currently see the best, but I'm still a little human."

"I know, but you know I'd be mothering you even if you were just here for a regular visit!" She was right too, Kendall always took care of me. She knew the life of a pilot and that I didn't have much to go home to, and tried to fill in where she could. Trip did the same. "I know you're tired, Dawx. We'll let you rest right after I grab your ice pack."

She returned with the cold compress and after a kiss on my good cheek, she and Trip went up to their bedroom, while I tried to get comfortable in the recliner. I could only hope my dreams were sweet and the thoughts of my future would go away, at least for the night.

CHAPTER SEVENTEEN

My parents had long gone to bed when Denny, Zak and I realized we had been playing cards until 3 a.m. Granted it was Saturday, and none of us had to work, but we had drunk the night away, and barely realized it.

"I haven't done this in a very, very long time," I said. "It's been fun."

"It really has," Denny agreed. Zak nodded and grabbed a few empty glasses, taking them into the kitchen, leaving Denny and me alone for a moment. "I've missed hanging out with you. And I think Dr. Zak has taken an interest in my cousin."

"Ha, I doubt that. It was just nice hanging out and being silly for a change. You guys gonna get an Uber back to your hotel?"

"Yep. The convention is over tomorrow. Well, I guess it's over *today* since it's so late," he looked down at his smart-watch. "We fly out later this evening."

"Quick trip," I said.

"You know how it goes."

"I do. When are you planning on visiting again?" I knew

75

the answer, and I shouldn't have asked the question, because it made him feel bad. He had no idea when he'd be back and I knew that.

"Soon. *Soon*. Promise. Let's try to plan some vacation time together, 'kay?"

"What's this I hear? Talk of vacation time?" Zak said, as he came back into the library. "Doctors don't take vacation time!"

We all laughed knowing it was probably true and a little sad at the same time.

"I've got to make it back here myself at some point. I'm jealous I don't get to enjoy this amazing beach." Zak's words were genuine and I thought about how fun it would be to have a beach day with the boys. Maybe if we ever could all get back together.

"You want to share a ride with us and we can drop you at home?" Denny asked.

"Nah, I'll go crash in the guest room for a few hours. I've got a house call tomorrow afternoon sometime, so I'll make it back home after breakfast."

Denny hugged me tight, and as I was walking the boys to the elevator, Zak reached out at the same time for a hug as well.

"I feel like we know each other and I'm a hugger." I didn't mind, and as soon as he enveloped me in his arms, I couldn't get his amazing smell out of my thoughts. Handsome. Check. Doctor. Check, check. And he smelled divine. Check, check, check. "Can we keep in touch?"

"I'd like that, I'm on Denny's social media and he can give you my number." I thought back to the familiar scene earlier with Dawson when we exchanged numbers. Two handsome guys in one day. I was on a roll.

"Sleep well, Vixie," Zak said, as he waved, heading toward their Uber.

"Love you, cuz!" Denny hollered back. I blew him a kiss and went back to the penthouse.

"I thought I'd find you in here," my mother said, as she pulled back the curtains across the huge set of windows, letting in the morning sun. I grimaced as the light hit my face, and I glanced over to see that it was already eight thirty. It was later than I expected she would have let me sleep.

"I know you're off your schedule, but I wasn't sure if you needed to get up at a certain time," she said, sitting down on the bed beside me.

I yawned and stretched before answering her, enjoying what felt like hotel sheets in the guest room of my parents' home.

"I have an appointment later this afternoon, but I don't have to work today."

"That's good. When you got here last night, I could tell you needed some rest. Want me to let you go back to sleep?" She reached over and scooted my hair out of my face, as she had done so many times when I was a child.

"Nah, I should probably get moving. Might take a bath in the garden tub before I go, if you don't mind." It was one of my weaknesses. A good hot bubble bath. And at my parents' place, the guest room had a tub with jets. Quite the step up from our childhood bathroom and the tiny shower in my apartment. Sometimes I wondered why I didn't just still live with my parents. They would have let me too. It's not like I was ever home to do anything more than sleep anyway, but alas, I had to be *independent*.

"How about I make you some French toast while you take a bath?" When she wasn't hounding me to settle down, *damn*, I loved that woman.

CHAPTER EIGHTEEN

I wasn't sure what I was expecting, but when Dr. O'Neale walked into the condo, she took my breath away. Tight jeans, and a black shirt that showed off all her curves... hell, her medical bag was even cute, and I was only looking at her with one eye!

I had to shoo Carter and Kendall away earlier that afternoon. I knew that Brucey had some kind of little league thing and they wanted to go. I was only by myself for a little while though, before the doc arrived, and that was the only reason they agreed.

She knocked and I was good to stay still, telling her the door was open, while not getting out of the recliner.

"Hey stranger, you're a sight for sore... eye, *ha!*"

"You too! You look rested! How are you feeling?" she asked.

"Kind of like a pirate, minus the rum." I shrugged my shoulders. I was wearing sweats and a white T-shirt, didn't see the need to get dressed up, but after she walked in, I felt a little underdressed.

"I was expecting to find Trip here with you," she said.

"I had to get rid of them. Kendall got my bed fixed up and stocked the fridge. He was going to sit down and watch TV awhile, but I knew they had somewhere to be, and would check on me later." Fuck, I was babbling.

"Oh that was very nice of them. And, to set you up here was genius." I explained to her Carter's connection to Silver Shores, and that his place was available. "Not that you'll need assistance, because I can tell you're the independent type, but it's good to know you can easily call and get it if needed."

"I guess I was expecting a Doc Baker experience, like from Little House on the Prairie, when you said you were going to make a house call," I confessed.

"I'm sorry to disappoint you! We've made a few strides in modern medicine since those days, though I have to admit I liked his medical bag." She was so cool and collected.

"Thank you for coming by today, so I didn't have to see one of your colleagues," I told her.

She asked me to lean the recliner back and she came over and gently un-taped the bandage. My cheek was the sorest part of all, and boy I could tell it was bruised.

"I'm going to turn off the light before I remove the bandage from your eye. The way you're lying, I don't want the light to be a total shock." Even during this at-home house call, her bedside manner was on point.

"You've thought of everything," I said... *except the fact that when you lean over me, your cleavage makes me want to pull you down for a closer look.*

"Alrighty, keep that eye closed for me once I take the bandage off, and then you can slowly open your eye."

She had pulled out some kind of wipe, and I could tell she was getting the crusties off where my eye had watered since the surgery. Doc was extra careful to make sure she didn't disturb the cut on my cheek.

"Open slowly," she guided me. Everything looked a little fuzzy, like I was in a fog. "Close your other eye so you can focus a little."

I did as instructed, and I felt kind of like I was in a dream, and she was floating above me.

"What color are my eyes?" she asked, wanting me to focus.

"I already know the answer to that," I said, but still complied. "I can indeed see they are a deep, ocean blue and I wouldn't mind getting lost in them." *Fuck, Dawson! You just said that to your doctor.* I wanted to facepalm and run away.

I was good at flirting, but this mouth of mine, when it didn't think, it was apparently *hella* cheesy.

"Yours are more of a steel blue, in my opinion." Regardless of my comment, her smile radiated across her face, and I liked seeing it.

Seeing it.

I was *seeing* it.

I opened both eyes and looked at her as we were still face-to-face, the realization coming over me like a douse of cold water.

"I can see." I blinked a few times and she backed up, so I could slowly sit up. "I can see you. It's still foggy, but it's coming back."

"This is very good news, Dawx," she said, using my nickname. The sound of it on her lips made me want her to say it again. "You're gonna have to stick strictly to doctor's orders though!"

And while I knew she was teasing a little, I knew I was going to have to be careful.

"Cold compresses, let's continue that for several days,

'kay?" she said, beginning to list off orders. "And the quick movements? None of that for a while. Your eye will be healing for the next two weeks at least. And drops. I'm going to put some drops in for you right now and they will continue for the next six weeks."

The doc had a prescription for me that I knew Kendall could easily get filled.

She explained that specifically because of my profession, she did not use a gas bubble procedure when repairing my eye, and hoped I would be flying sooner rather than later, but I knew that would all depend on how well my vision was restored.

Vision requirements for flying meant I needed about 20/40 vision without correction, but I could wear glasses or contacts as long as I got to 20/20 vision with them. It was a narrow margin, and I had never taken my good sight more for granted than right now.

CHAPTER NINETEEN

Not only was he alone when I got to Silver Shores, he was wearing gray sweatpants and a tight white T-shirt. If Victoria's Secret made lingerie for men, he'd have been a runway model.

I appreciated he had been following my orders and keeping his head still and propped up. It was one thing patients had such issues with, because it was so out of the norm. That and eye drops. You'd think they were killing people with as many complaints as I had received over the years.

"So now what?" his question caught me a little off guard. Normally, I'd have a nurse go over the things we had just talked about and take him to check out.

"Well, later this week, I'll look at my schedule and get you an appointment for another follow-up." I could tell by the look on his face he appreciated it, but didn't know what we were supposed to do next. I also didn't like the idea of just leaving him alone to fend for himself. "Can I take a look at your cheek?"

He nodded and I came closer to get a better view. I

grabbed my medical bag and changed the bandage, cleaning up the edges around where the cut had been glued together. On a jagged edge, Dr. Rass had actually used a couple stitches where the skin had been broken badly. I hadn't seen this up close until now.

I noticed the whole time I was looking at the cut, Dawson was staring into my eyes. He really could get lost in them. I hated seeing his pretty face all battered and bruised. His cheekbone would forever have a little scar from the cut. I thought about how he would tell stories about it, and it brought a smile to my face.

"What is it?"

He noticed.

"Ha!" Now I had to tell him. "Oh, I was just thinking about how you'll woo all the ladies with this badass scar you're gonna have."

That comment brought out his million-dollar smile, and I liked the sight of it. I finished up on his cheek and stood from the armrest of the recliner.

"What else can I do for you before I go? I'm very handy, and not just as a good doctor."

"Ha! I'm sure you are very talented. You're great at planning pancake breakfasts too." He wasn't wrong. "What's on your agenda for this afternoon? If you're not busy, we could order some food? It's the least I can do."

I thought about how this would never be something I'd do with a patient, but then again, I didn't think house calls would be either, and of course, my brain went to worrying about him being alone, *and lonely*.

"I am free tonight. And tomorrow, oddly enough. I finally put my foot down on working too much, and set a meeting with my manager on Monday to talk about some reduced hours." I felt like I was defending a dissertation.

"I'm proud of you. Doc. Kaleb said you worked a lot, so this is going to be good for you." I appreciated his support.

"Alright. Well, if we're gonna hang out, I'm going to take off my doctor hat, and we're just gonna be friends, 'kay?" I could tell he started to nod his head and stopped

"Takes some getting used to, the whole not moving... but yes, I'd like to be friends."

I held out my hand. "Vixie."

"Dawx. But you already know that," he said, and winked his good eye, tightly shaking my hand. I was going to have to figure out how to stop staring at him. If I had been out with friends and saw him across the bar, I would have had the same reaction, and hoped he took notice. He was definitely my type, if there ever was one, but what girl wouldn't say that?

Dawson was in his prime. Twenties looked good on a man, but thirties looked even better. There was no more baby fat on this specimen of a fine gentleman. His cheekbones were chiseled, his arm muscles wriggled when he flexed his hands. God knew what he was doing when he made Dawson Kaczmarek.

"So, what are you in the mood for?" I asked, pulling my hand away. I held onto his a little longer than I should have, but the contact felt good.

"To watch or to eat?"

"Ha! Both, but let's order food first."

"You are the local. I am only in Boca a couple times a year when I have a layover and am able to visit with Trip and Kendall. So, you tell me what's good?"

"There's a pizza and wing place nearby that's good. We could order from there?" He liked my suggestion and I looked up their menu to read to him what they had. We opted for a pizza and some boneless wings to share. He figured he could heat up the leftovers for lunch the next day.

"I'm not up on my pilot regulations. What does your vision have to be to clear you to fly?" I asked, needing to know if he was going back up in the air.

"Think I'll get there?" he asked, after telling me all the specs.

"What was your vision the last time you were tested? 20/20?"

"Better actually. 20/15." I grinned, knowing he would likely pass the required sight test. "How good are my chances of getting back up in the air, Doc?"

"Can't make any promises, but I'm hopeful for you. And it's Vixie, remember?"

"Vixie. Yes. Tell me about your beautiful name and how you acquired it."

"Mom and Dad are Max and Vickie," I said, and shrugged my shoulders.

"That's so cool. You're one of a kind, even in your name... now that I think back, you told me this in the E.R., while I was inebriated..."

"Ha! I did! But you didn't tell me how you got your nickname. Why do people call you Dawx?" I mean, we were sharing, so it seemed like the time to ask.

"Oh. Well. Pull. Up. A. Chair." He scratched his head and I burst out laughing.

"Is it that bad?"

"Heh, you're gonna want to settle in for this story..."

CHAPTER TWENTY

"So I know a little Polish," I explained, gently kicking the feet up on the recliner as Vixie slid her shoes off and curled up on the couch. "And if you were unaware, the Polish word for commander is dowódca... daad-oud-ka... stretching it out when you say it is important to the story."

"I can't wait to hear why." She smirked and rested her chin on her hand, intently listening.

"One night way back in the day when I was still trying on my baby pilot wings, I was out at a bar with the guys... and we were very drunk. So, I decided it was an opportune time to start speaking a little slurred Polish." *Gawd, why was I telling her this*? "I think that's enough. This story is way better when Trip tells it and I can go hide my head in shame."

"Nope, you're not getting out of it now, spill the rest!" Vixie was fixated and the embarrassment was about to begin.

"Well, I referred to myself as commander in Polish... *daad-oud-ka*, but I kinda slurred it together with my first name and called myself Daad-oud-son, which apparently at the time sounded like I was howling—not that I remember it, mind you, this is just what they tell me—all the while meaning to say I was the commander."

I paused and watched her contain her laughter, which she was doing very well.

"My friends, including that good buddy Trip, thought I sounded like a dog and they started calling me *Dachshund* instead of Dawson... which eventually got shortened to just Dawx."

"Commander Dawx. Do they call you this on the plane? Like the flight attendants, do they call you *commander*?" Her teasing made me want to rush her, and if she licked her lips again while she said my name again, my eye healing would be the least of our worries.

"You wound me," I said, pretending to be injured.

"No, seriously, like what do they call the pilot? I've heard both captain and pilot." She masked making fun of me by changing the subject.

"Captain is standard. When you begin to taxi, the captain usually says a little greeting to the passengers and introduces himself as such, but the captain is in command of the aircraft, so commander is often interchanged."

"Fuck, you just turned into... like, a serious pilot." Her response caught me off guard. "Sorry. Can't help myself sometimes when I take off the doctor hat."

"I dare say the word fuck isn't ever going to bother me, I just might have been caught a little off guard by the fact that it came from your sweet lips." *Which she bit. Right there. Staring at me while she did it.*

What a fantastic time for the doorbell to ring. The food arrived right as I was unsure where that conversation was supposed to go next. I was also thankful Vixie hopped up to go get the door, so I wouldn't have to and I wouldn't have to explain why I was flirting with my doctor. I mean, *my friend*. We were acting as friends, right?

"This place is fully furnished, how cool is that?" Vixie said from the kitchen, where she was opening up the takeout containers.

"This used to be Trip's bachelor pad," I explained. "And the food smells amazing!"

I slowly sat up, getting better at watching my quick movements. I noticed my arm was resting exactly where Vixie sat earlier when she was checking out my cheek.

I wanted to be near her and prove to her I could follow doctor's orders and take it slow. It was the first time I had stood up and walked around since she had taken the patch off of my eye too. And it felt weird.

My depth perception was correcting and I was thankful I could see for the most part. It was still foggy, but I was sure it had improved in the little time it had been since she added the drops.

"Want to eat at the table, or back in the living room where it's more comfortable?" she asked, and turned to find me a few steps behind her. "Whoa, you're sneaky like a cat, I didn't even hear you. How's the vision?"

She reached out and steadied me placing her forearms under mine as if they were little handlebars. Her touch was electric, and every time her skin was on mine I felt a jolt, a shock I longed for again and again.

"Vision is still a little blurry, but getting better."

"The drops will help too as you have more doses. I'll be sure to help you with them again when it's time in a couple hours."

She planned on staying a couple hours.

Okay.

This was good.

Now I had to figure out if this sexual tension was just one-sided, or if there was the possibility of something more with my doctor.

CHAPTER TWENTY-ONE

His arms.

Against my arms.

I wasn't sure who was steadying who.

And I had just invited myself to stay a while longer.

The little angel on my shoulder was shaking her head at me, while the devil on the other was pulling out her pom poms.

He's my patient for fuck's sake.

"I wouldn't mind actually sitting at the table and getting out of the recliner for a minute if that's okay with you?" Dawson said, while not letting go of me.

"It's good to see you up and about," I said, and slid around out of his grip to take the food over to the table. "You're also taller than I guess I was expecting."

Come on, Vixie. Small talk. Stop being awkward as hell.

"Shame we don't have any beer to go with this pizza. Kendall grabbed a few things for me at the store, but she said I had to ask you first if I was gonna be taking any medications that might not go well with alcohol."

"She's a smart woman," I said, opening the pizza box

and grabbing a couple plates and napkins to put on the table. "I'll take care of all this if you want to get comfy."

"You don't have to wait on me." I knew it wasn't an order, more of an *I-can-fend-for-myself* plea, but I still wanted to take care of him.

"You, my new friend, will have plenty of time to fend for yourself, so let me help while I'm here."

"Yeah, I told Carter he had the night off. Figured I could tuck myself in... but his persistent texts mean he'll be over first thing in the morning."

"I'm glad he's here for you in Boca. With your injury, you need a place to stay put for a bit, and it's good your friends are here to help."

The wings were delicious, as usual, and we had ordered a pizza I hadn't tried before too, and I liked it as well.

"You'll have to leave the number for this place. It's good food and convenient delivery," Dawson said, resting his chin on his fist as he ate. I could tell he was tired.

"I didn't give you a prescription for pain medicine or anything to help you sleep, but I can if you think you need it," I said, watching him play with his food.

When we were standing together so closely in the kitchen, I really hadn't taken into account how tall he was. He had always been in the hospital bed or in a chair. I realized how his arms would envelop me if he hugged me and I got lost in the thought of that opportunity.

"...so yeah, Trip and I have gotten ourselves into a pickle a time or two, but we never tried any kind of drugs, pain medicines, or sleeping pills for fear they would mess us up and we wouldn't be able to fly." I came back to reality around the end of his conversation, pleased he was such an adult with those kinds of decisions. I had gathered that alcohol was their vice, when they had the time to enjoy it.

When we finished, I took care of the few dishes and stowed the leftovers in the fridge for another time.

"So, how can I make you more comfortable?" I asked, knowing I had a plan already.

"Come sit down? Hang out?" His questions felt like pleas, and I had full intentions on doing just that, but I had a quick errand to run.

"Gimme ten minutes and I'll do just that?"

"Oh... kay..." He was definitely questioning my plans as I slid my shoes on and squeezed his hand.

"Just gonna run over to the drugstore real quick," I explained. There was one pretty close to Silver Shores, conveniently located, for all the residents. I went ahead and sent in his prescriptions for eye drops, and wanted to pick up some Extra-Strength Tylenol, since I now knew he didn't have any.

But, mainly, I wanted ice cream.

It was one of my three guilty pleasures. Bubble baths, which I had already had that morning. Coffee. And ice cream. Even better was coffee ice cream while taking a bubble bath, but I wasn't picky.

Two pints of Ben & Jerry's and his medicine and I was back to his condo.

"I was wondering what you were up to, you didn't have to get my drops, but I appreciate it," he said, as he met me at the door.

"You didn't have to get up. You should be keeping that head still," I fussed.

"I know. I was already up for a quick trip to the bathroom while you were gone. It's hard not being the gentleman."

"Chocolate Therapy or Urban Bourbon?" I asked, holding up the two pints.

"Fuck yes. Ice cream! I love ice cream even more than pancakes!"

If I didn't already have a crush on this guy, he was melting me even further with his similar affection for frozen treats.

"Since I can't have beer yet, how about I eat some bourbon-flavored ice cream?"

"Excellent choice," I said. "I thought that being from Kentucky you might pick this one." Grabbing two spoons, sliding off my shoes and heading over to the couch as promised, I took the lid off our pints and settled in.

"What shall we watch?" he asked, and slid the remote over to me. "There's like a million streaming services available, cable and on-demand movies."

"This place *is* fancy."

We settled on A Few Good Men, and fell silent as the sun went down, and we devoured our ice cream.

"Hey, Dawx?"

"Hmm?" he said softly.

"I never said you couldn't have alcohol... just go easy in your condition. We see where it got you the last time, 'kay?" I couldn't help but smile.

"Does that mean you'll bring a couple bottles of wine when you come over for dinner tomorrow?"

Smooth, wingman. Real smooth.

CHAPTER TWENTY-TWO

Sleeping while sitting up was so not my jam. I was a tosser and a turner and this restrictive sleep wasn't getting me much rest. At least with the hospital bed, I was able to recline a little bit more than I could on the couch or recliner.

I had discovered the Silver Shores recliner options were either straight up or completely flat. Vixie was a doll and helped me get my pillows set, so I wouldn't move around too much while I slept, and I was able to get comfortable. She curled up on the chaise lounge in the bedroom and we watched more TV and talked until bedtime.

Bedtime.

Yeah, after the eyedrops and a couple Tylenol, I completely dozed off.

It wasn't until Trip and Kendall arrived with breakfast that I realized I had slept all night in the same position. My neck was stiff and I had crusties in my eyes.

And, to my surprise, a sweet, beautiful doctor was curled up, sound asleep still in the chaise lounge next to me.

"Oh, gosh! We're interrupting," Kendall said, when she

saw both of us in the bedroom. She started to back up out the door when Trip came up behind her.

"How ya feelin' today, bud?" He stopped in his tracks when he saw Vixie too, and the commotion woke her up. "Jesus, if I'd have known you needed someone to stay with you, I'd have come back!"

"Oh. Whoa. Sorry. Totally didn't mean to fall asleep," Vixie said, immediately pulling her hair into some kind of bun thing, and looking around for her shoes. She was still wearing my hoodie, which swallowed her whole, and the sight couldn't have been more perfect.

"It's okay. Everybody calm down. We *are all* adults here." I started to sit further up in the bed, slowly, and looked around for my own T-shirt. I had tossed it off at some point in the night, since I usually slept without one.

"Drops," Vixie said. "Want me to help with those before I go?"

"I really would," I admitted, as the peanut gallery watched from the doorway. "Hey Vix?"

She stopped fidgeting long enough to look up at me. "Hm?"

"It's all good. It's no problem at all. *Really*. Don't mind the audience over there."

"Let's give them a sec, Trip," Kendall said, and tugged Carter into the living room with her.

"I *so* did not mean to fall asleep!" she mouthed at me, once they were out of earshot.

"I'm glad you stayed." I held onto her arm as she came over to put the drops in my eye.

"These are like an antibiotic, and though it may feel like they are lubricating your eye, in between drops, it may feel dry. I got you some other drops to help with that if you need them," she explained, and changed the subject.

"So... you're gonna come back later and help me with these drops again? I'm kinda helpless you know..." I stuck out my bottom lip and she bit hers, shaking her head.

"You mentioned something yesterday about wine, so I guess I better come prepared?"

"I shall work on ordering something fantastic to go along with it," I snickered, as she stayed in my arms, even after she was done with the eye drops.

"Sounds good to me," she agreed. "Here, let me take off your hoodie. You might want it later."

"Or maybe you will? I enjoyed spending time with you yesterday. I hope you did too."

"Still not sure about this whole doctor/patient thing, but yes I did."

We were just about face to face the way she was standing at the side of my bed and I certainly didn't want to risk it being the wrong thing to do, but I couldn't help myself and pulled her face to mine. Her lips were soft and she didn't pull away. She smiled into the sweet kiss and kissed me back. No regrets there.

"Hey Vixie?" She leaned her forehead against mine. "Can I shower now, or do I need some kind of eye patch thing?"

Back to reality, unfortunately.

But I was not going to stink when she came back later that evening.

Even if I had to take a whore bath, I'd figure it out.

"I forgot... I brought you a waterproof patch so you can shower. You just want to make sure you keep water and soap out of your eye, so be extra careful when you wash your hair." She ran the knuckles of her first two fingers along my jawline and went into the living room to get me the patch. "Had it in my bag."

"Thank you, I'm looking forward to a shower." What I wanted to say was I was looking forward to a shower *with you*, but I wasn't gonna push my luck.

"I'm going to slip out. Text me later and I'll come back over. 'kay?"

"'kay, can't wait."

She headed out into the living room, where I heard her say a few things to Trip and Kendall, and get her shoes. I leaned back on the bed, and waited for them to come in with all their questions once the door closed, and Vixie had left.

"Dude!" Trip said, on cue. "Did she stay for a medical reason, or just because you wanted her to?"

"Calm down, I'm fine. We watched several movies last night and talked until it was really late. I'm not surprised at all that she fell asleep."

"So, you're okay then?" Kendall asked, already straightening up the bedroom.

"Yep. Just a little tired. And I probably need to take a couple Tylenol."

"I can get those for you," she said, and went into the kitchen for a glass of water.

"Thanks, Kendall." I looked over to Trip waiting for more grilling. "She knows I can do that right?"

"Yes, but you know she likes to baby you." Trip picked up my T-shirt off the floor and tossed it at me.

"Sure, you're okay?"

"Actually, I'm *better* than okay..."

CHAPTER TWENTY-THREE

"Hey, Mom." I put my cell phone on speaker.

"Hi honey, just checking in to see if you're still planning on swinging by tonight for dinner?" *Shit. I forgot.*

"Mind if I take a raincheck? I forgot about something else that has come up..."

"They called you in for another shift, didn't they?" *Not exactly.* "I hope you can get all the extra hours straightened out soon. You work too much, honey!"

"I know, Mom. I've actually got a meeting with management tomorrow morning to discuss," I explained.

"Well, try to get some rest, dear. We love you." My mother's sentiments were genuine, even if they were because she and my father wanted different things for me.

I stopped at my favorite coffee shop, just down the street from my place, and ordered my usual drink and a mini-quiche.

Sundays, or the day off I had before working for several days in a row, were typically the day I used to get ready for the week ahead. Where I was in and out of the E.R. so much,

I typically wore hospital-issued scrubs, but I did take care of laundering my own coats.

I also tried to rest up as much as I could and restock my groceries. It was very typical of me to only have frozen meals, coffee, water and ice cream at my apartment. I almost always ate a salad at the hospital, because there was no telling when I'd get to eat fresh produce at home, and after the shifts I took, when I got home, eating wasn't number one on my list.

So shower, groceries and laundry were on my list before heading back to Dawson...

The door was open when I knocked and heard Dawson say, "Come in!"

I didn't pack an overnight bag, I wasn't going to be presumptuous, but I wore comfy, yet still cute, clothes in case we had a repeat night. One good thing was I would always have clothes to change into at work and I never went anywhere without my medical bag.

I laid down the bag from the grocery on the counter and went over to see how he was doing.

"Sight for sore eyes," he said.

"Occupational hazard, but that eye of yours is gonna be sore for a bit." He grinned at my joke.

Dawson was freshly showered, his hair still a little damp and obviously just tousled with his fingers. Tight T-shirt again, and a new, darker pair of grey sweatpants. He could see the big breath I inhaled when I settled next to him.

"Fuck, you smell good." His grin grew even bigger.

"I like it when you're Vixie instead of Dr. O'Neale... you're comfortable enough to say bad words around me."

I giggled. "Gonna put my doctor hat back on for a second though... let me see that eye."

"Do normal patients get this many checkups?"

"Are you normal?" I couldn't help it. "I promise I won't charge you a co-pay. Lemme see." He did as instructed and let me get a good look at him. "Did you do your midday drops okay?"

"I mean. No. I got it all over my face instead of in my eye, but I'd say one drop got in there at least." He shrugged his shoulders.

"Since I'm here, allow me to assist," I told him, and added in some of the lubricating drops, hoping that would ease some of the dryness I knew he had to be feeling. "How's the cheek?"

"It would be better with a kiss." *There was that smooth wingman again.*

"It would?" I scooted further over and sat down on the arm of the recliner. "That's not a prescription I write very often."

"You said it yourself, I'm not a normal patient." He turned his cheek out toward me and tapped his bandage three times.

"Normal is far from what you are, but I'll oblige..." I gently kissed just below the bandage on the skin of his cheek. I couldn't help but linger for just a second, breathing him in, feeling the stubble along his jawline against my own cheek.

"I'm feeling better already!" he said and winked his good eye.

"You may need further treatment later, so be sure to keep your doctor abreast of the situation."

I got up and went to the kitchen, unpacking the bag I brought in from the grocery.

"Wine," I said, holding up two bottles. "And... ice cream."

"You're a peach, you know that?"

"I did not get peach ice cream. Do you like that one?"

"Not particularly, you've got it covered just being you."

"Good 'cause there was a sale on Häagen-Dazs and I'm stocking up your freezer." I had brought over six pints to get him, well us, through the week. I didn't have ice cream every day, though I wanted it daily. But, I did plan to continue checking on Dawson if my schedule allowed it and he wanted me to, of course. "What did you decide on for dinner?"

"I was thinking street tacos? There's a place not far that delivers and Trip recommended."

"Sounds great and will go great with the wine I brought."

My cell phone rang.

"One sec," I said, and picked up. "Hey Martina... yep, thanks for calling, just wanted to check in and see if we were still meeting in the morning?"

"If that's okay with you, I've got you down at 9 a.m.," she said.

"That'll be just fine. I haven't received a new schedule for the month yet, and usually do by now, can you let me know when I'm working?"

"Doesn't look like you're scheduled until Wednesday, I'll double check why you didn't get your alert like usual. I'm sure something is wonky in the system." *Always was.*

"Just knowing that helps a ton. I'll check in after we meet tomorrow and figure out the rest of the week, thank you!"

I hung up, pleased with a couple more days off. It was the whole reason for meeting with Martina in the first place, but I knew I'd probably get called in sometime before that, because somebody else was out.

"Everything okay?"

"Yep, I have a meeting with my manager tomorrow, so all is well." I was kind of excited to talk to her about working less, so I could make a plan for the future.

"The heart of standing is that you cannot fly."

- *William Empson*

CHAPTER TWENTY-FOUR

She even brought ice cream.

I had hoped to see her bring in a bag with a change of clothes, but I didn't want to assume anything. After all, even though we had been calling ourselves *friends*, she was still my doctor. I probably needed to take it easy on my eye too. And chill out a bit.

Kendall thought it was funny when I asked for her to bring over some coffee the next time she came. She knew I rarely drank the stuff and assumed it was for my *new friend*.

I had also figured out that the local grocery store had delivery, so I'd be doing that instead of bothering Kendall and Trip when I needed or wanted things.

Vixie and I were deciding on what to order for dinner, when there was a knock on the door. I didn't mean for it to startle me, but being so unexpected and banging so loudly, it caught me off guard and I jerked my head.

"Oh, Dawx!" Vixie said, and got up and came to my side. I put my head in my hands, an instant headache coming on, and she took care of the door. "Sit tight."

"Can I help you?"

"I'm Diana, the patient aide assigned to Mr. Clyne's condo..."

"Come on in, Diana. Please, knock a little softer next time, you gave us quite a jump." Vixie coming to my rescue again.

"I just wanted to swing by and introduce myself, see what I could help with... I'll be working until Thursday, so I'll check in every once in a while to see if you need anything," she said.

"Nice to meet you," I said, my head still in my hands. "I'm good for the night if you want to come back tomorrow. My *friend* is here to help." I didn't get a good look at her, and frankly didn't care at that moment.

Once she replaced the towels in the bathroom, Vixie showed her out, telling her I didn't need my sheets changed.

"I gotcha, Dawx," she said, once she closed the door. Out from the bathroom she came with a cool cloth and laid it over my eyes, then closed the curtains and dimmed the lights. She got some peppermint oil out of her bag and put a drop on the temple of the good side of my face.

"Be back with some Tylenol. You haven't had any recently, have you?"

"Not since early this morning," I told her. "I didn't know they had nurse aides."

"*Patient* aides," she corrected me. "*Diana* doesn't need to provide you any type of care. If you need something, you need to go through the actual nurse."

Boy she got protective really quick.

"I'm glad you clarified, didn't know the difference."

"Exactly why I explained," she said, and squeezed my shoulders. "Lie still for a few and that should ease up."

"You're really good at this whole taking care of me thing," I admitted. The cool cloth on my face and the smell of the peppermint helped ease the pain and I thought about how Vixie nicely brought to the aide's attention not to bang on the door.

"I think we had the taco business figured out when she came in, so I'll go order."

"Grab my wallet," I pointed aimlessly, without moving my head. "I mean it. I'm buying dinner."

I could tell she was mocking me, even though I couldn't see her face. I also liked the idea of her walking around my place barefoot.

"So, this headache coming on like this was fun and new." The sarcasm in my voice was laid on thick. "This gonna be a thing for a while?"

"Yeah, you'll get headaches off and on. Some worse than others. But you have to remember, even though your vision is improving, you just had eye surgery, *and* a substantial blow to the face."

"You're right. I get it. I'm just impatient. I'm used to being able to go and do as I please, and this is cramping my style."

"I never would have guessed, *Commander*."

Oh, that tone in her voice was hella sexy. I wanted to remove my cold compress but refrained and listened to her order our tacos.

"I'm gonna put this wine in the fridge so it can chill for tomorrow. I ordered a couple sodas to go along with our tacos..."

"Sodas...?" I whined.

"Yeah... doc's orders. I'd rather you take it easy with this headache coming on."

I knew she was right, but that didn't mean I liked it.

"So, does that mean you're coming back for dinner tomorrow night?

"I swear, I think you must like my movie picking or something."

"I do. And I like your company."

She told me about her morning meeting with her manager and that she didn't think she was on the schedule until Wednesday, but gave me a tentative yes.

I wasn't doing too bad taking it slow after all.

CHAPTER TWENTY-FIVE

"I'm going to see you later, right?" he said and wrapped his arms around me. A few kisses the night before and we had settled into a casual chumminess.

"I'll text you for sure after my meeting, 'kay?" It was taking a lot of restraint on both of our parts to keep it casual. I didn't want to do anything that might jeopardize his healing process, and neither did he as there was too much at stake.

I was looking forward to seeing Dawson again later on and was getting a little too comfortable on the chaise lounge in his bedroom.

Arriving at the hospital early, I grabbed a coffee from Kisha, and stopped by my locker to change into scrubs. It would be more professional than the casual clothes I wore to Dawson's place and had on for twenty-four hours.

Martina was her perky self when I arrived at her office. "I wasn't expecting you in scrubs on your day off, come on in!"

"Force of habit, I suppose!" *Well, kinda.*

"What can I do for you, Dr. O'Neale?"

"Honestly, I just wanted to see if you could reduce my on-call hours a little. Where we have been so busy lately, my call ins have been extremely regular, and I end up working a full shift."

"Oh wow, I'm glad you brought this to my attention." I could tell she was glancing at my hours. "You're not actually getting in many days off... which could lead to some labor issues. Thank you for letting me know." Martina was the Manager for the physicians in our hospital, since we were contractors. There were enough of us she was able to procure an office in the building to provide better support, and we all appreciated that she was close by.

I knew there was a science to scheduling and I sure didn't want Martina's job. We chatted for a bit in her small, hidden-away office and I couldn't get my mind off getting back to Dawson. The smell of his cologne was in my brain and I needed to breathe him in again.

"While I've got you here, let's get your schedule fixed up for the month, and talk a little about your long-term goals. So, where do you see yourself in five years? Honing your specialty, looking for a private practice maybe?"

Was she serious? Like I would tell her I had a tiny thought about doing my own thing.

"My father always says emergency medicine is the most rewarding. Being able to help those when they are most in need." It was true. He did say that, but the longer I worked in emergency medicine, the more tired I became. Part of that, I'm sure, was the constant scheduling and working. I needed a mental health break and a chance to figure out what the hell I wanted to do with my life.

"It is a very fulfilling profession, most definitely." She typed as we talked, not sure if she was actually listening to me or not. "You know a lot of this is automated, so it evens out hours... would you want to add in any extra vacation time coming up? You have a bunch saved."

"Actually..." I thought about Dawson and his window of recuperation. I didn't have to tell him I purposely planned vacation time...

"I think I need to meet with the Director too as we may need another full-time or at least another part-time ophthalmologist to keep up with the load.

"Thanks for coming in, Vixie!" I preferred to be on a first name basis with Martina, and was glad she embraced that, even if I did have to give her a look for calling me doctor earlier.

I was headed to the locker room to get out of my scrubs when an unfamiliar text tone caught my attention.

Good morning, beautiful.

Not who I was expecting.

Not who I was expecting at all.

It was Denny's friend Zak.

I just about dropped the phone. I didn't actually expect him to reach out. Much less with a *beautiful*. It took me a second to figure out how to respond.

Good morning, handsome.

Real original, Vix.

Despite how captivating Dawson was, and how I had just planned time off to be with him... with any luck on his part he'd be back in the skies in less than a month and I'd be back to business as usual. It only made sense to keep my options open, and Dr. Zak McIntyre was most certainly *an option*.

"I read somewhere that flying is like throwing your soul into the heavens and racing to catch it as it falls."

- *Linda Howard,*
Mackenzie's Mountain

CHAPTER TWENTY-SIX

Good news, I'm off until Wednesday for sure. Not on-call either.

Her message was just what I needed. Not that I couldn't handle being alone, I was just limited on what I could do, and having company made me feel better.

I'm sure Kendall would have hung out, but I didn't want to impose and ask her. Trip was on an overnight trip and he said he'd be back to visit Wednesday, so the week was looking good.

Be serious. Do you want me to hang out with you the next two days? It won't hurt my feelings if you don't.

Aww, it *wouldn't* hurt her feelings? I had hoped she was just being polite.

I need some serious help eating all this ice cream, so uh... yeah. I want you to hang out.

We texted back and forth for a bit, and she volunteered to actually cook dinner, which was fine with me. I rarely had home-cooked meals. I'd devoured the last of Kendall's tiramisu and enjoyed every bite. I was thinking about asking her to make me another one after all of Everett's wedding festivities were over with.

That was something else I was hopeful for... that my doc would release me to go to the wedding as long as I was careful.

The patient-aide lady caught me off guard, yet again, by banging on the door. I was glad that I refrained from reacting like I had the last time and kept another headache at bay.

"Come in, Diana," I said, resting my head on the back of the recliner cushion, closing my eyes.

"What can I do for you today, Mr. Clynes?" she asked. Hell. I didn't know what she could do for me. And I wasn't in the mood to explain I wasn't Mr. Clynes. That also told me she hadn't been working here for long.

"I'm not entirely sure. What do you do for other guests?"

"I replaced the towels in the bathroom and kitchen area..." she started to explain.

"That would be good, thank you."

"I change the linens on the bed and sometimes help with showers or baths or dressing." Diana was a lip smacker and had a huge piece of chewing gum in her mouth. That I could tell with my eyes still closed.

"I won't need your help with those things today, but thank you."

"I can also do a little cleaning and vacuum your floors."

"The vacuum might be a little loud for me, but if you wouldn't mind if I stepped out for a few minutes, I'll take a walk while you do it."

"That'll be no problem, sir. Give me about fifteen minutes and I'll have this place spick n' span!"

I went into the bedroom to find my sunglasses, baseball cap and wallet and headed outside.

"I've got my key in case you leave before I get back," I told her. "Thanks for your help."

A walk would be good. So would a breath of fresh air. A partly-cloudy stroll was just what I needed.

As I put one foot in front of the other, I thought about how she offered to help me bathe. News flash to Diana. *Nobody*, other than my *new friend*, would be helping me shower or dress. Just the thought of her assisting made me wriggle.

I came upon two residents sitting at a bench in the open area of the community. I tipped my hat and planned to leave the greeting at that, until one of them cat-called once my back was turned. I just couldn't let that go.

I did a slow about face and went over to sit right smack in the middle of them, spreading my arms across the back of the bench.

"Ladies. I don't think we've been introduced?"

"Not formally, but we know who you are..." the one on the left said.

"You do?"

"Carter's pilot friend."

"And you two princesses must be Muriel and Bertha?" I assumed, but knew I was probably right. Trip had told me about these two ladies and they were exactly how he described them.

Lady number one sat up on the bench and reached over me to swat her friend. "Did you hear that Bertha? He knows who we are!" *Ah, now I knew which was which...*

"I heard him just fine, lady." She swatted her back.

"Well, tell us your name, Pilot. Or shall we just call you Captain?"

"Captain is a little formal, don't you think? I'm Dawson Kaczmarek, and my friends call me Dawx."

"Oh, that's a sexy Polish name. Say it again!" Bertha jiggled with delight.

I obliged, not able to control the smile they caused. "Kaa-ja-mar-eck...Dawson Kaczmarek."

"Dawx is pretty cute too," Muriel chimed in. "You got a lady friend? 'Cause we could be your friends."

"I can always use more friends," I said, and winked under my sunglasses.

"So, what're you in for?" Bertha made it sound like I was in the slammer. We chatted for a bit about my eye and they told me the scar on my cheek would be sexy once the bandage was gone. They were rather entertaining and enjoyed that I called them princesses.

"Will you come play Bingo with us on Thursday night? We can sit just like this and make a pilot sandwich!" Muriel's offer was kind, and I thought about needing to get out, especially while Vixie was away.

"I can't say for sure I'll be able to read the cards with my eye still healing, but I wouldn't mind the company." They practically squealed.

"Muriel, it'll be just like when Carter came to play Bingo, only this time we're not sharing *Dawx*," she said, and clapped her hands a couple times. The inflection on my nickname was sweet too. I had a feeling I was going to like these two ladies.

"What do you like to eat, honey?" Bertha asked, and further explained they loved cooking for Carter, but he was rarely around much anymore. If they were going to insist, I sure wasn't going to be picky.

"Now that we know you're settled, we'll swing by and see our Prince," Muriel said, and she and Bertha excused themselves to the community room. I decided to walk a little more before heading back to the condo.

It had turned out to be a beautiful day.

CHAPTER TWENTY-SEVEN

"Where'd you sneak off?" I asked curiously, when Dawson came into the condo. Diana had been vacuuming with the door open when I arrived, so I just came on in.

"Went for a walk while that aide-lady person was here. Didn't want to have to talk to her or listen to the vacuum."

"Aww, such a social butterfly," I teased. I was unpacking groceries when he came over and kissed my cheek.

"I like that ballcap and sunglasses. Sounds like a suggestion your doc would make to keep the light out of your eyes."

"I do try to follow my doctor's orders... couldn't stand for her to be mad at me..." he said, and teasingly swatted my behind and walked over to the other side of the counter to sit on one of the barstools.

"Steaks, eh? I like steaks."

"Me too, I figured this would be a winner. Hope you like Brussels sprouts and baked potatoes too."

"Brussels. Sprouts." He looked at me like a child who was planning on finding a way to feed his vegetables to the dog.

"You don't like Brussels sprouts? How old are you? Do I need to check your license?"

"Hehe, maybe! I never liked them as a kid. I'm not sure I ever tried them again." He shrugged his shoulders.

"Alright... two bites and if you don't like them, you don't have to eat anymore, but you have to promise to try them!"

"Okay, deal. What do I get if I eat three bites? Maybe you'll take off that little tank top of yours? Can we play strip Brussels sprouts?"

"Have you already forgotten I like them? You'd be naked pretty quick..."

"Maybe we'll just keep score and save that game for later..."

I got a Caesar salad kit to make life easy and slid it across the counter to Dawson with a bowl.

"Can I trust you to put that together?"

"Yes, ma'am," he said, and took on his task with more energy than I had seen him have in a while.

We had a quiet dinner and finally opened the wine. We discussed shows we liked and tried to find something neither of us had seen to watch later in the evening. Movie watching with Dawson had become a favorite pastime, and I thought he had been enjoying it too.

"Can I come over there and sit on the couch with you?" he asked, shyly.

"It ain't called a loveseat for nothing!" *Oh my, did I just say that out loud?* It made him smile, BIG! And he slowly made his way over to sit beside me.

"Oh, wait..." He stopped in his tracks. "It's ice-cream time."

Two pints and two spoons later and we were snuggled on the loveseat. My legs were comfortably in his lap under a teal throw that Kendall had bought along with Dawson's new bed set.

I could get used to this.

"Tell me about becoming a doctor," Dawson said, out of the blue. "Did you always want to do this, or were your original career goals world domination and being cute?"

"Ha, no, I never wanted to go into the medical field growing up. The only child of a doctor though, it sorta picked me."

"What does your Dad do?" he asked.

"Well, he's technically retired now, but not really. He retired from working in the hospital to doing consulting more on his own," I paused to take a bite of my strawberry ice cream. "He was the Chief of Staff at a hospital in Miami for... shoot... longer than I can remember. When I went to college, they moved up here to Boca, and I managed to find a job close by."

"That's awfully short, sweet and to the point... I feel like I'm missing some important parts of your journey to becoming a superheroine."

"I leaned on my parents for a long time, knowing they were going to pay for my education, and continued to support me all through college. I didn't have it in me to break my father's heart and go into fashion design. The money is probably better in medicine too. Thank goodness I was smart enough."

"Of course, you *are* smart enough," he chimed in.

"Can I have a bite of yours? I've not tried that flavor... need to know if it's any good."

Dawson's smirk told me he had plans to more than share.

"Irish Cream Brownie is definitely a flavor I approve of, and I don't mind sharing..." He took a bit of ice cream on his spoon and slowly brought it to my lips. I opened my mouth and he fed me the ice cream slowly, allowing me to savor the new-to-me treat. As he pulled the spoon away, Dawson deliberately trailed a drop of ice cream down my chin.

"Oh, oops... let me get that," he said, and leaned over, gently licking the excess from the corner of my mouth, following the trail until he had taken care of the "spill."

His lips were warm, a total contrast from the ice cream, and I wanted more of his kisses.

"That's better," he said, and sat back up. *Fucker was a tease and he knew it!*

"So what kind of doctor is your father?"

Okay. I can play that way while you pretend to change the subject.

"He's a cardiologist. Doesn't practice anymore really though. He consults and helps practices and hospitals with organization and speaks at conventions and conferences."

"Sounds like a pretty good gig."

"Yeah. I think he enjoys it. He wanted me to go into cardiology too, but I preferred the eyes."

"The eyes, eh?" He turned to look at me square.

"Yep. The eyes." I started to take another bite of ice cream, when I decided to return the favor. "Want a bite of mine?"

Dawson nodded and I scooped a big spoonful of the pink treat up on my spoon. I gestured toward his mouth, but turned the spoon and took a bite myself, leaving a little ice cream on my bottom lip.

"You'll have to come and get it," I said, and shrugged my shoulders.

CHAPTER TWENTY-EIGHT

Until now, I wasn't sure how much more of this slow-burn business I could take, but the ice cream tease had pushed me over the edge. I didn't give a second thought to her tease and went straight for her lips. I was hungry for Vixie, and the soft growl from deep within her belly told me she wanted me too.

"I ate my Brussels sprouts," I whispered into her ear right before I nipped her soft skin.

"Uh huh. Yep. You did."

"So what's my prize?"

"Whatever you want... just remember, you just gotta take it easy," she said, barely making out the words. *Always the doctor.*

She took the ice cream back to the freezer and shed her pink top on her walk back to me. The see-through tank top was on my list to get rid of next.

My usual hookups were nothing like the experience I was having with her. I had actually gotten to know more than just her first name and favorite drink. And come to think of it, I didn't even know her favorite drink.

"I really like your grey sweatpants..."

"These old things?" They *were* comfortable.

"Mmm hmmm," she grumbled, and straddled my lap, kissing me hard and fast.

"If you *were* a cardiologist, I'd tell you that you've given me a *heart-on*... but you're not, *so* you can just feel what's happening underneath these sweatpants you like so much."

"*Eyeeee*, can feel it," she joked back, and reached down my stomach to slide my shirt over my head. She took care not to mess with the bandage on my cheek, nor hit my eye with the fabric.

I took the liberty to take that little tank off too, and unclasped her bra with my other hand.

"Mmmm. Skin to skin." Her touch was addicting as she worked her way up my neck, rubbing her tits against my chest.

"Self-control, 'kay? Can you handle it?"

"I'll make myself."

She rose back up and strip-teased off the rest of her clothes, while not breaking eye contact. Oh, how I wished my vision wasn't still foggy. The sight of this beautiful, naked woman towering over me was a view I needed to be clearer. She tugged at the band of my sweatpants and swiftly tossed them on the floor.

"Here? On the couch?"

"We'll make it to the bed later. Plus, you gotta keep your head up."

Oh, fuck, honey. My head was up.

"Lean back, close your eyes, and let me..."

"Let you, whaaa?"

I was pretty certain at that moment it was likely not a good thing for my eyes to roll back in my head, but when she went down on me, there wasn't anything I could do to stop it. The hiss I took of air confirmed to her she was pleasing me.

"You okay?" she stopped to ask, ever the caregiver.

"Yep," I gasped, not meaning to, but no other words were needed, and she went back at it. *Lord Almighty*, she was going too fast. I wanted to have *her*, too.

"Vix. Wait." She stopped. "Come here."

She brought her face back up to mine and kissed me sweetly. Knowing her mouth had just been making love to my dick, and now was kissing me like there was no tomorrow, made me hornier than ever. She was insatiable. I started to lift her onto my lap and she stopped me.

"That's not taking it easy. You're gonna have to let me command tonight, pilot." I surrendered easily. At that moment, she could have done anything she wanted to me, and I'd have let her without question.

"Birth control?" I felt like a douche for even asking.

"Yeahhh..."

Just in time too, as she straddled my legs again, easily lowering herself, until I was inside her completely. She held herself there, allowing us both to feel completely full for just a moment before she firmly dug her short nails into my shoulder blades, and used me for stability.

Up.

Down.

Slowly.

Feeling every *sensation*.

The goddess was on top of me, and we were face to face, eye to eye. Holding onto her waist as she slid back and forth was exhilarating, like looking into her soul. Her mess of hair all over the place, her motions pleasing us more and more as she led.

I was proud of myself for letting her take charge without

protest. *Don't get me wrong, I enjoyed every minute of it*. But, I was *used to* being in charge.

There *was* one thing I could do that I didn't think would cause too much strain, or get me in trouble with the doctor...

I steadied her with my left hand as she continued her grind, sliding my right hand down my stomach, meeting her clit with my fingertips. She let out a moan, and I wondered if the neighboring residents could hear us. Beyond curiosity, I didn't care.

"More?" I asked. She had thrown her head back with pleasure and nodded. *She liked that.*

"Mmm, Dawx. *Fuck.*" Yeah, I was pushing the right button.

I continued rubbing in a circular motion and could barely hold off any longer.

"When you come... I'm gonna come."

"Yesss," was all she could mutter, and a few seconds later, her orgasm came like a fireworks display. She held onto my biceps with all her might, and I couldn't help but watch the show before me as I came hard too, pulling her even closer to me and tight against my cock. I could feel every muscle, every inch she moved, and every sound she made.

She lay on my chest, nestling her head in the crook of my neck while I was still inside her. We lay that way, breathing each other in for a few minutes in silence.

Vixie finally sat back up, kissing my lips like it was the first time, letting me taste her and enjoy her sweetness.

"Hey, girl. You okay?" I asked, as she got up, and excused herself to go to the bathroom.

"Never better, Dawx. *Never better.*"

CHAPTER TWENTY-NINE

I came out of the bathroom to find Dawson on the couch, only wearing his sweatpants, still sweaty and hella sexy.

"I could get used to this view... shame I can't see it better." He closed his strained eye to watch me walk naked through the room with a better sense of vision.

"In time, patience, my *friend*," I said, looking for my clothes that had been scattered all over the floor. I slid on my panties and found my tank top. At this point, there wasn't much to hide, and I think we both realized we could be comfortable.

"Let's finish that ice cream, shall we?"

"It's like you know me," I said, and went and retrieved our open pints. "Whatcha wanna *do* now? Movie? Talk?"

"Talk. If that's okay? Can't really see the TV well anyway, so it's more like listening to shows than watching them."

"Talking is good. I rarely get to socialize these days, unless it's in passing with a friend at the hospital."

"How do you take your coffee?"

"All sorts of different ways." Well, it was true. "My 'usual' is a skinny cinnamon roll latte at the shop in the hospital.

The barista there knows me and I have a tab, she also knows several drinks she makes that I like." That was a facepalm moment, I was a little snobby with my coffee, but Dawson seemed to understand.

"I get that. You work a lot and weird hours. I'm sure caffeine is your friend when you need a pick-me-up." He was right.

"Same with you too, I would assume." I had curled back up next to him on the couch, tossing the throw back over my legs. Dawson had inhaled the last couple bites of his ice cream, while I was savoring mine. I thought he did it on purpose though, as his next move was to find his way under the cover, and rub my legs with his hands.

"Yeah, caffeine is my friend, but I've never really been a coffee drinker. Couldn't find a way that I liked enough to have it more than once. So, I stick with Cokes and energy drinks."

"Is that what's in your cup while you're flying?"

"Yep, and a bottle of water too. I try to balance it out. Gotta keep this stunning physique of mine." He smirked and patted his toned abs.

"I'd say there are other ways you keep those abs in check."

"Crunches and sit-ups probably do the trick."

It was nice having an adult conversation with no agenda. I looked over and saw the screen on my phone had lit up from a message.

"Gotta make sure it's not the hospital," I explained, though Dawson needed no explanation, he knew about my commitments.

It wasn't the hospital.

It was Zak. I left the message unread and went back to Dawson. *Be in the here and now, Vixie.*

"Everything okay?"

"Yep! No emergency."

"So the other night... was *I* an emergency?"

I couldn't help but giggle. "You were indeed."

"I'm so sorry they called you in for my dumb ass." His apology was sincere.

"I'm not. I'm glad they called me back in. Yes, I had already worked a lot that day, but your well-being is much more important than a few hours of sleep."

"You're the real deal, Dr. O'Neale."

"You ain't so bad yourself, Commander!"

"Can I interest you in snuggling on my state-of-the-art hospital bed, complete with designer sheets?"

"Well, if you're not a smooth talker! I'd love to!"

He led me into the bedroom as if I had never been there before, and we raised the top of the bed, so Dawson could keep his head elevated.

"It's gonna feel so good to lie flat again."

"Yes, it will, you'll feel a little more normal then." I got his pillows situated and slid in next to him, spooning his side and laying my head on his chest. "If my crazy hair gets in your face, I'll put it up."

"No, it's fine," he was petting my neck, and I wasn't taking for granted how much I was enjoying his company.

"Hey, Vix? Think it would be okay for me to go to a wedding on Saturday?"

"You'll be a week post-op at that point, so it should be fine. Is it a beach wedding?"

"I think so. A pilot buddy is getting married... the one we were celebrating at the bachelor party when the uh, incident happened."

"You'll take it easy?"

"I will take it easy. And... you're off on Saturday?"

"I am..."

"Soooo, you'll be my date?" We hadn't moved from our snuggling position through this whole conversation, and even though he couldn't see my face, I knew he could tell I was smiling.

"I'd love to... as long as you promise to sport those Ray Bans in case it gets too bright for you, 'kay?"

"Always taking care of me..."

CHAPTER THIRTY

"Dawx, buddy! I'm back in town. How are you? How's your vision?" It was good to hear from Trip.

"Vision seems to be improving a little each day, and while you were away I have managed to charm the ladies here at Silver Shores."

"Ah, Muriel and Bertha come to check on you?" Couldn't fool him.

"They made the most amazing pot roast, and Vixie and I ate it twice there was so much!"

"Vixie, eh? What's going on with the doc?" I assumed I was about to get a lecture, but I didn't care.

"Err, yeah... we're having a nice little fling. Not sure what it'll lead to, but enjoying each other's company, nonetheless."

"You sound happy, man. Different, but in a good way."

"Not gonna analyze it, at least not yet anyway." This was not a road I wanted to travel at the moment. I didn't want to ruin what we currently had going on, because it was good. *Real good*.

"So, how about I come getcha and bring you over to the

129

house, and we barbecue this evening? Kendall is just about ready to head to the store to grab some stuff, whaddaya say?"

"Sounds good to me. Vixie gets off at seven, unless they need her to stay longer, care if she drops by?"

"I'm down," he paused, and I heard Kendall in the background say, *"Ask Dawx what he wants for dessert!"* "You hear that? The boss wants to know what you want for dessert. Hey, why do you get to pick the dessert?"

"'Cause I'm charming? Tell Kendall to surprise me, maybe something with peanut butter?"

"Fucker," was the term of endearment that was returned to me and made me chuckle. "Anyway, I'll come get you about four and we can hang, how about that?"

"See you then, man."

I sent a quick text to Vixie and she responded that she'd meet me over there when she got off work. I'd decided to take a quick walk before coming back and showering, when Diana banged on the door. *Gah,* I felt bad for the other residents if she banged that loud for them, but then I wondered if some couldn't hear her. Whatever. I was getting used to just staying out of her way.

"Come on in," I said, opening the door for her and stepping into the kitchen, so she could go by with her cleaning cart. That morning when I got up, I had sent my bedding to be laundered, and she returned with it to make the bed. Kendall's purchase of expensive sheets definitely made my stay nicer.

"I'll make your bed, sir, and replenish your towels, and vacuum. Can I do a quick spot clean for you too?" she asked, as she rolled on into the bedroom.

"Yes, thank you. I was just about to get a little exercise, so take your time." I started to leave the condo, when I realized

I needed to grab my hat and sunglasses. "I have my key, so please lock up when you leave."

"Will do, sir."

Silver Shores was a beautiful complex and the residents were super nice. Trip, and now his pilot friend—aka me—were the only ones under retirement age to take up residence, and boy did they treat us good. His history had served us well. I wondered if he still wore his pilot uniform to emcee Bingo on Thursday nights. I would get to see firsthand when I joined Bertha and Muriel for a little O-69 action.

They had made and brought over so much food, and even came in and kept me company, while Vixie ran home to get a change of clothes. When I got back into my regular routine, I planned to stop by and see my new friends as often as I could.

An unexpected phone call stopped my leisure.

"Hey, Aunt Faye," I answered. Faye Kaczmarek was my father's sister and my favorite aunt. She still lived near Spring City, Kentucky, where I grew up, and where my father was currently residing in an assisted living community, much like Silver Springs.

"Hi, honey, how are you?" It wasn't like her to call. She would text me now and again, but rarely called unless something was wrong.

"I'm... uh... I'm doing fine, how are you? How's Dad?"

She proceeded to explain to me that his dementia had been gradually getting worse, which I didn't think was possible, but every now and then he had a lucid spell, and asked about me.

"I don't know if you'll have any time off soon, but it might be good to visit," she said. "It's really been years since I've noticed Colt having any semblance to himself, but here lately I've been visiting and he's recognized me, and even asked about you. The caregivers mentioned it to me too."

"I thought you said his dementia was getting worse, so how is he recognizing you?" I was confused and worried all at the same time.

"Well, that is confusing, yes dear. When he's not having a spell where he remembers—which isn't more than once a day and for a short period of time—he's worse... sometimes violent... sometimes he forgets to eat... sometimes he cries, and sometimes he hollers and they have to sedate him. Sweetie, the doctor fears he may not have much time left."

Her words hit me like a ton of bricks. It had been years since I visited my father, but every visit I did manage was to a stranger. It broke my heart that he didn't know me, but at the same time it also tore me up that I put such a burden on Aunt Faye by not being around.

"I'll see what I can do," I told her. I knew flying wasn't an option for at least a little while longer, but I wasn't sure how much time he'd have left.

I'd have to talk to Trip and Vixie and come up with a plan to get to Kentucky.

CHAPTER THIRTY-ONE

A dinner date.

With his best friends.

The invitation made me wonder if we were just having fun, or if Dawson had even thought through what was happening with our little fling.

I was thankful for an easy day at work, but dreading the potential call in after I left. It always seemed to be busiest in the evenings.

I would have made something to take over to Trip's house as a nicety for the invitation, but there wasn't much time for that. Instead, I planned to swing by the liquor store on the way over there and grab something, maybe a local craft beer or seltzer.

I sent Dawson a text when I was on my way. Right before I left, I grabbed a tear-off eye chart from one of the storage rooms. We'd often give them to patients who needed to work on focusing, and Dawson was about to be one of those patients.

I was thankful for my good change of clothes being in

my locker where I had left them just in case. Cute T-shirt, jeans and sandals could be worn just about anywhere.

"Hey, sight for sore eye!" he said, when I arrived at Trip's place. "Only one is sore at the moment, as you know."

"Punny. Punny." I handed him one of the two six-packs of assorted beverages and carried the other one inside.

"Hey, Doc!" Trip said, as he was walking from the kitchen out back.

"Hello again, glad you could come!" Kendall said, from the sink. "Dawx, go put those on ice. Thank you for the drinks, you most certainly did not have to bring anything!"

"I appreciate the invite." I really did. It was kind of weird going to a *patient's friend's house*, but I had to stop thinking of Dawson as my patient. I wasn't done being his doctor yet though. I shook my head at the thought. Once he was healed up, I'm sure it wouldn't be as awkward.

"How was your day? Those jeans are cute," Dawson said. "Hugs all the right spots. Can I hug all the right spots?"

"Later..."

"Does that mean you're coming over after we're done here?"

"Maybe..."

"Playing hard to get this evening? I like it."

"Indeed. How are you? How's your *sore eye* as you call it?"

"It's the same. Still blurry, but seems to be getting a little better every day. Or I'm just getting used to it."

"I brought you a poster to put up, so you can start judging how well you're seeing out of that eye. It'll hopefully help you heal faster. Like eye exercises."

"You saying I need to exercise?" His teases made me want to bail and take him straight home.

I reached down and whispered in his ear, "I thought you wanted to see me naked?"

"Yup. Better exercise. Yeppers."

The spread of food was way too much for the four of us. Brucey, their son, had eaten earlier since dinner was kind of late, which I blamed on them waiting for me. It was a nice adult evening though.

"Next time we'll light up the fire pit," Trip said, "...and roast marshmallows. I didn't think the smoke would be good for Dawx though."

"He's a keeper, Dawx," I said to Dawson, and winked at Kendall.

"This barbecue chicken is amazing, Trip!" Dawson ignored my sentiments and grabbed another piece from the platter.

"It's the brine and the killer homemade sauce Kendall makes. She's the real winner here."

My phone in my pocket buzzed. It was Zak. I hadn't responded to his last text, so I'm sure he thought I was ignoring him. Well, I *was* ignoring him. I didn't want to message him back around Dawson. Didn't seem right.

"I think you'll like dessert, Dawx," Kendall said. "I can package it up for you to take home too if you're too full."

"Tell me more," he said. I too, was interested in what she had made.

"It's a peanut butter banana pudding. Made with Nutter Butters and a peanut butter whipped cream on top."

"Good lord, woman. You're a goddess in the kitchen."

"Well, we haven't tried it yet," she snickered.

When we finished dinner and she started to get our dessert, I decided to get up and answer that text message.

"I'm gonna excuse myself to the restroom and I'll come back and help you with that!"

135

"Just down the hall, first door on the right," Kendall said.

Hey, sorry. I've been swamped. How are you? I messaged back.

I finished up quickly in the bathroom, and went out to do something in the kitchen, so I wouldn't feel like such a freeloader. She had already served up dessert and was back on the patio, so I went to join them.

And as soon as I sat down my phone buzzed. He would just have to wait. I wasn't going to be rude.

"You okay, babe? You look a little flushed."

"Yep, just a doctor thing. All good." At least it wasn't a complete and total lie. He was a doctor. I just felt like a cheater for even talking to him...

I had to talk to Dawson, so I could figure out what it was that we were *doing*.

Was this a fling?

Was it more?

I felt like pulling my hair out of sheer confusion.

CHAPTER THIRTY-TWO

When we opened the door to the condo, I knew immediately something was off.

"Hang on a sec," I said to Vixie, holding my arm out to tell her to stay behind me in the doorway. Trip's Louisville Slugger was leaning up against the wall, and I grabbed it ready for whatever might have been in the bedroom.

I appreciated the fact that Vixie actually listened to me and stayed still as I crept through the open space.

"Anybody there?" My tone wasn't nice.

Nothing.

I flung open the door to the bedroom and the screen door was ajar. Whoever was in the condo was now long gone.

"It's okay, Vix. Whoever was here isn't now..." I pulled out my cell phone to call Trip.

"Hey, man, somebody has been in the condo. Just wanted to make sure it wasn't someone you sent before we called the police."

"No, definitely not. I'll be right over."

He didn't live far away from Silver Shores and I appreciated his quick reaction. I looked around to see if anything might've been out of place.

The dresser drawers had obviously been opened and ruffled through, and so had my now-empty suitcase. It didn't appear they'd found the secret compartment in the bottom of it, where I kept my personal documents and my passport, which was what I was most concerned about.

"You and I are going to take a quick stroll down to the reception desk, while Trip heads over here... just want to make sure it wasn't Silver Springs personnel before jumping to conclusions."

We told the receptionist our discovery, and she called the night manager, who immediately went to check on staffing.

"It shows here Diana cleaned your unit earlier today, but no one else is on the schedule, especially not in the time frame you said you were away..."

Vixie noticed through the large window that Trip had pulled in and was parking, while we were in the front office. She went out to meet him, and I let them know that we would be calling the police.

"It doesn't look like anything is missing," I told him. "But then again, I don't see as well as usual and I didn't really look more than just what we saw on the surface."

The officers that came by checked the place before we went back in, and the manager verified that the keypad on the door hadn't been used, so whoever had been in the condo came through the sliding glass door.

That I apparently left unlocked.

Even though I hadn't opened it.

Yeah. Weird.

"I'd like for you to have the door rekeyed," Trip told the manager.

The whole thing was just suspicious.

"Who would even know you're here to break in?" Vixie asked.

"I dunno. Maybe it was just some kid being nosy, looking for money or something," I said. "I really don't think anything has been taken."

"They didn't get to your ID or passport or anything, did they?" Trip asked.

"Nope. Still zipped up and secure."

Vixie's phone buzzed and I nodded for her to step out and take the call. She was probably needed at the hospital.

"Thanks for leaving the baseball bat here," I told Trip as the officers were leaving.

"I had it in my hand as we were moving your stuff in the other day, didn't think a thing about it and forgot to grab it when I left. I'm glad too!" We looked around some more, and once everyone else had left, I told him we were fine, and said good night.

"I'll check in tomorrow. Kendall will be out helping with wedding prep since she's a bridesmaid, so I'll be around the next two days."

"Sounds good, man. Oh yeah..." *I had forgotten to tell him...* "I'll have a plus one on Saturday if you could tell Everett."

Trip snickered as he left. Vixie came back inside the condo and locked up after him.

"Well, this was weird," she said, with a smile and raised eyebrows. "Are we good now? Are you okay? A little rattled?" She was good at deducing my feelings.

"Yep. Got a new keycard and the back door is closed up tight."

"That all that's bothering you?" she asked. *I wanted to ask her the same thing.* She seemed off the whole time we were having dinner.

"Actually no. I got a phone call today that has me a little shook up."

"What's going on?" she asked, and brought me a beer from the fridge. "I'm gonna turn the A/C down a little and come sit on the couch, so you'll have my undivided attention."

I slid off my shoes and sat with her. The companionship of just having another human next to me was nice. No sex involved. Just a friendship. Being there for one another. I didn't realize how much I had missed it, until it was right there rubbing my arm, and telling me it was going to be okay.

"I need to tell you a little history, before I tell you about today's phone call, so it all makes more sense if that's okay?"

"We've got all night, Dawx. I'm not going anywhere."

CHAPTER THIRTY-THREE

Dawson's situation with his father in a nursing home, and losing his mother at such a young age, really made me appreciate my parents, and how *normal* I felt.

"Okay, so the obvious mode of travel is out of the question—but you already knew that. You really need to wait at least another week before flying, and maybe even a little longer than that."

I didn't want to lecture him, but I needed to be his doctor at this very moment.

"Yep, no flying."

"And while you're probably okay to drive, it's not a good idea. It's too long of a trip for you to do it on your own. You're going to need to rest."

"Yeah... thought about that too."

"I'd been meaning to tell you this, but I guess it just didn't come up in conversation or, errr... well, I dunno I just wasn't sure what we were doing, but I've got a week off of work beginning Saturday. The meeting Monday went well and she offered me some extra time, so I took it. Never look a gift horse in the mouth, right?" Fuck, I was rambling. "So, if you want the company, I can drive you north."

"Really?" he paused for a minute, and I was afraid I had stepped over the line. We still hadn't discussed the elephant in the room about what in the world we were doing. "You'd hop in a car and drive me all the way to Kentucky and back?"

"I love a good road trip! And, I have been enjoying your company…"

"Me too. Both I mean. And you're right, we haven't discussed what exactly it is that we are doing, but I hope it's not going to end when my eye heals up?" And that was discussing it. I didn't want it to end. But how in the world would we make that kind of long-distance relationship work. Timing his layovers with my shifts at the hospital would be a nightmare.

"Let's just keep doing what we're doing then… and see how it goes?"

"Is it time for ice cream?"

"After Kendall's amazing dessert? You still want ice cream?" *Was he just trying to appease me?*

"Kinda, yeah!"

"I've got something in mind I think you'll like, gimme just a sec." I ran out to my vehicle to grab the eye chart and my measuring tape I kept in my bag, and hurried back to the living room.

Carefully measuring out twenty feet from the wall, I laid the baseball bat down on the floor as a marker. I had spied some tape in one of the kitchen drawers and hung the poster up on the wall in front of the bat.

"Are we setting up shop? You gonna start taking appointments here?" Dawson teased.

"Only for one *particular* patient," I said. "Now, wait for

it." I jogged over to the fridge and grabbed a pint of ice cream. Classic vanilla. Perfect.

"I feel like you're up to something."

"Yep, come stand behind the bat. For every line you read correctly, I'll give you a bite!"

"Hmm, I'm game and ready for your shenanigans... this sounds way better than Brussels sprouts." He stood where instructed and started reading with his good eye, carefully covering the other with his hand. "E."

"Ha! You want a bite for the top line? Fine. I'll give you that one," I said, and spooned out a bite of ice cream and fed it to him. "Next line."

"F. P." He waited for his next bite. "T. O. Z."

"You're doing great," I said, and took a bite for myself.

The big letters were easy and I knew he'd ace the first eight lines with his good eye, no problem.

"Hey now. You better make sure there are enough bites for me to finish my game, I'd hate for you to run out and have to improvise."

"That, my dear, was exactly my plan...switch eyes."

"E. Bite?" I complied. "F. P. T. O. Z. Two bites?"

I lifted the spoon to his lips for the first bite and raised up on my tippy toes to nibble his lip while he practically inhaled the ice cream. Trying to pull me in for a kiss, I leaned back and shook my head.

"Fourth line. Focus," I said. He rallied and focused, unable to lose the grin while he concentrated.

"Okay. I got this. L. P. E. D... bite?"

"Good job. Yes, bite." I lifted the spoon to his lips again and he bypassed it, going straight for mine. Dawson kissed me hard and fast. I didn't want to break the kiss, but our game was important. I needed to see how far he had to go.

143

"Bite rejected?" I pulled away and ate the ice cream. "Bite for me!"

"Fine!" he squalled like a little kid whose toy had been taken away.

"Next line."

"P. E. O. F. D." He was squinting and working hard to see the letters.

"Try the next line for me. Just see what you can make out," I instructed. He had mistaken the C for an O on the last one, I knew he wouldn't get the next line right.

"F. D. L. C. F. E. D."

"Good try. Bite for effort."

I lifted the spoon to his mouth for the last bite, kissing the vanilla off his lips.

"I made a follow-up appointment for you to come in and *officially see me* this Friday. Your cheek is healing nicely and the Dermabond will continue to dissolve, but we can get those two stitches taken out while you're in the office."

"Oh, I'll come see you Friday," he agreed, and I knew he was wanting more, because I was too.

CHAPTER THIRTY-FOUR

"Thank you for the ice cream," I said, and grabbed Vixie by the waist, pulling her toward me.

"You did a good job on your eye test. We will keep working on focusing and it'll get better as you heal."

She stopped me to go grab my eye drops, so we wouldn't forget. I was still terrible at putting them in myself. Ever the doctor caring for her patients.

"Think we're gonna get there though?" I asked, still in the back of my mind worried I might never fly again.

"We're gonna get there, Dawx. *You're* gonna get there. Have a little faith."

"Right now, I just wanna get you, can we do that?"

"Can I shower first? I usually shower after a shift, but didn't have time, so I just washed up and changed before coming to Trip's for dinner," she said.

"Can *we* shower?" Okay, so maybe I was being a little facetious, the woman wanted to clean up for me. That in itself was a nice gesture, but I didn't care how dirty she was, I just wanted her.

"Yes, *we* can, come on..." She took my hand and led me

to the bathroom, our fingers interlocked as if *I* didn't know the way this time.

Vixie pulled the curtain closed and turned on the water. "Sorry, buddy, I have to insist on the eye patch if you're getting in here with me."

"I will, sweetheart," I said, and pulled her top over her head. She was already unbuttoning her tight jeans and shedding them to the floor. My clothes were coming off just as fast. I had plans for her before we got in the shower, and she was moving faster than I could keep up with. She started to step inside and pull me along with her, but I knew she was waiting for me to put on the eye patch to keep my eye covered. "Wait."

I pulled her to me, our naked bodies flush and warm from the steam of the shower. I tipped her chin in my direction and tasted her lips, like the most indulgent ice cream, not being able to get enough of her. I nibbled kisses down her jawbone to the nape of her neck, sliding her arms around my neck, and hearing a little moan as I hit a sweet spot just below her ear.

"Wrap your legs around me," I instructed, and lifted her onto the bathroom counter. She was at the perfect height for me to hold her close. Her clawing my shoulders and arching her back had me aching for her. "I need to be inside you, I can't wait for the shower."

She didn't protest, in fact she slid closer to the edge of the counter, and opened her legs as an invitation. I held off just long enough to kiss down her breasts and stomach, stopping at her belly button, nipping the skin to get her attention. I travelled further down, licking and sucking and teasing, until I found her sweet spot.

Catching her off guard, she tossed her head back against the mirror and ran her fingers through my hair, pulling my face into her sex. It was exactly where I wanted to be at that moment, treating her to the euphoria she had given to me over the past week we had known one another. I licked and sucked her clit into my mouth until she was unable to keep quiet.

I couldn't wait any longer and stood tall, sliding inside her easily. She was wet for me. And warm. And *mine*.

"Don't overdo it, Dawson." She could barely get the words out, but our lovemaking wasn't a strain. It was sensual and relaxed, and everything it should have been.

"I'm good. I promise," I whispered in her ear, pulling her to me so I could dive deeper and slide harder. Pushing her over the edge into an intense orgasm made her moan and dig her nails into my back. I could feel her wriggle around me and I came as she came.

"Don't let go yet," she said, before I pulled away. I held her tighter, and for a few minutes we stayed glued together. I felt the connection we were finding with one another, and I hoped she felt it too.

"You have an early shift in the morning?" I asked, as we made our way to the shower.

"Yep, and probably a long night as well. I got the feeling today that the other doc wouldn't be around tomorrow evening."

"Well, we better wash up so we can go christen that fancy hospital bed of mine, before we get you tucked in..."

"You're insatiable."

"And that's a problem?" The sarcasm was real.

"Nope, not at all..."

"At 30,000 feet up
The mind has plenty of space to wander"

- *Eugene Redmond*

CHAPTER THIRTY-FIVE

I was right about the fact that I'd be working late at the hospital. I had the hunch and hit the nail on the head. I hated missing Bingo night at Silver Shores, especially knowing Trip would be the emcee, but it would be good for Dawson to have some time alone.

On my lunch break, I had made an appointment to meet with a financial advisor about the potential plans for me to open my own practice. With the right planning, and if it worked out, I could still take on shifts at the hospital, but then refer patients to my own practice, instead of other places. Patients like Dawson weren't ones I wanted to let go to other doctors, I wanted to see their care through, and didn't always get to do that.

Hell, who was I kidding? There weren't other patients like Dawson. But there were patients that I thought were special.

The day dragged on, and I spent a little time with Kaleb, helping where I could. Not that I ever wanted to see a full E.R., but time sure went by faster when we had things to do, and the evenings were when admissions picked up.

The surfer who had face planted into some coral was my biggest issue of the day. He ended up being okay, but it took quite a bit of time and cleanup to make sure his eye was alright. Like Dawson, he was lucky.

Zak had been texting me on and off, and I wasn't sure what to say to him. We made small talk. Getting to know you questions. All harmless and things I'd ask any girl-friend, but just the idea that I was talking to another guy made me feel guilty. I ended up telling him I was taking a much-needed vacation, and planned to turn my phone off for a week. Ridiculous, I knew, I had zero intentions of doing that, but I needed to turn Zak off for a week. He seemed to understand.

You work hard, you deserve to unplug.

Thanks, buddy. You're not wrong.

After Dawson hit the two-weeks-post-surgery mark, I'd have a better idea how his eye was healing, and he'd likely get back to business. Then we'd know where the road would lead.

"Hey, Mom, you caught me on a break," I said, as I was walking down to the coffee shop to grab an afternoon pick-me-up.

"Oh, good, dear. Denny called and said you were on vacation next week, and I hadn't heard a word about it, so I thought I'd check in. Do you want to have a girls' day?"

"Uh, yeah about that..." What in the world? Zak had told Denny I was on vacation, and Denny called my mother? "Had a few vacation days saved up and the schedule opened up, so I decided to take them."

"Well, what are you planning, dear? Surely you're not going to just sit at your apartment for a week? Though, I wouldn't blame you if you did, you work too much."

"Gonna take a little road trip actually..." And I knew she

was going to fish the information out of me, so I just decided to tell her before she tried, "...with an old friend from college. Just gonna get out of town for a bit and unwind."

"Alrighty, honey, keep me posted so I don't worry. Denny said something about you planning to turn off your phone."

"My goodness, Mother, you seem to know more about my plans from Denny than I do. Gotta go, talk to you soon." If I could have slammed the phone down I would have, but cell phones were too damn expensive.

"How's it going, Doc?" Kisha said, as she handed me a cup of happiness.

"Just got off the phone with my mother," I said, and rolled my eyes.

"I completely understand," she said, and laughed.

"Kisha, I have a question for you," I said. The thought hit me that I had no time before Saturday's wedding to find something to wear, and I *was not, under any circumstances* asking my mother. "I need a dress to wear to a wedding on Saturday and I have about an hour later this afternoon to find one. Do you know of any little boutiques or shops around here that I might be able to find something in a hurry?"

"Oh, yes, girl, I do..." she said, and pulled out her phone to show me a couple hidden gems that weren't far at all from the hospital. One was in walking distance, so I wouldn't have to find a parking spot, which was extremely helpful. "Beach wedding?"

"Aren't they all around here?"

"Ha! You're right! Usually they are!" The sweet girl suggested a few types that would flatter my body type and she made sure to tell me to find some sandals that would be easy to slip off for walking on the sand.

"Next time I need a personal shopper, I'm gonna call you when I have more time on my hands, 'kay?"

"I got you covered, Dr. O'Neale!"

Thank goodness somebody did!

CHAPTER THIRTY-SIX

"Isn't he dreamy?" Muriel said over me, as Bertha laid out the Bingo cards in front of us.

"Who, Carter?" I asked, knowing she wasn't talking to me.

"No, Mr. Sandford, who's snoring over there in the corner, of course Carter!" If the lady didn't feed me as well as she did, I might have sassed her back, talking like that over the top of me. *Ew, Carter. Dreamy?* I cringed a little.

Silver Shores official Bingo night was still emceed by the one and only Pilot Carter Clynes, when he was available. The ladies seemed to drool over the man in uniform, his top two buttons open, and his captain's hat cocked sideways. Hell, he *was* kind of dreamy. If the eye thing didn't work out for me, I could explore the male escort scene. Hunky pilot, that I could do.

"Can you see the cards okay, honey?" Bertha asked. I could, they were close enough that it wasn't really a problem, and doing as my doctor suggested, it was a good way to do my focusing exercises.

"Getting there, vision is a little better each day," I said, and smiled at her.

"So, did you figure out who broke into your place?" Bertha asked. I should have known that word would travel fast around the community.

"Nope, not sure at all what that was about. Doesn't appear that they took anything though. All my stuff was trifled with, but nothing seems to be missing."

"But did they get any of your information? Identity theft is a big deal these days, and people are always trying to scam us old folks, because they think we don't know any better," Muriel said.

"Yep, we took a seminar on how to prevent that!" Bertha chimed in.

"Here's a favorite, ladies and gentlemen," Carter called out over the speaker, interrupting our conversation, "Lucky seven!"

The ladies marked all their cards and some of mine I had missed. I was obviously not paying much attention.

Their question about what kind of information they could have taken had me thinking. If they had found my hidden pouch in my suitcase with all my important papers, they could have taken anything they wanted, but it didn't appear they had. There was mail on the dresser, some opened, but I didn't believe anything had my social security number on it. I had my wallet with me that night, so that was safe from prying eyes. I started to dismiss the thought when I realized my discharge paperwork from the hospital was sitting on the dresser with the mail and would have all kinds of information on it.

"Did that class you took tell you what to do if you think somebody has stolen your information?" I asked, purely curious at this point. Who knew if Muriel and Bertha could help me any further with this thought or not.

"Sure did, we'll tell you all about it tomorrow over lunch," Bertha said. She and Muriel were serious about their Bingo skills and the eye candy at the front of the room wearing the cocked captain's hat.

"I'd love a lunch date," I agreed, and let them play my cards while I watched Carter work his magic.

"Doctor's orders, y'all!" he said, like he knew what he was talking about.

"Which one is that? And how does *he* know all this stuff?"

"He learned the lingo years back... it makes it more fun," Bertha said.

"Doctor's orders is for the number nine. Back in World War II, army doctors gave out a pill by that name to soldiers..." She hunkered down next to me to whisper the last bit, "...it was a laxative!"

My two tablemates broke out into laughter over that and others in the room did too. They must have known the lingo too and that my friends had to explain it to me. *Did I even want to know the meaning of the rest?*

As I was sitting there in the midst of a room full of senior citizens, I realized I was missing Vixie. Everybody had their significant other or best friend, like Muriel and Bertha. I flashed forward and hoped when I was their age, I had someone sitting beside me playing Bingo, and loving life together.

There weren't many days I was brave enough to think about the future as I was always trying to live in the moment, wherever I ended up laying my head that night. I tried to enjoy my travels, but I was realizing I was missing out on other aspects of life. The thought was kind of scary.

The ladies continued marking my bingo cards, and I put my arms behind them, letting them eat up their pilot date for the evening. I should have worn my captain's hat, so they'd get to brag to their friends.

CHAPTER THIRTY-SEVEN

I told Dawson I'd probably just crash at home, or at the hospital after my shift, depending on how long I had to work. I immediately regretted it, knowing I didn't want to be apart from him anymore than absolutely necessary, but I knew we needed some boundaries. I'd see him Friday anyway, mid-morning, for his appointment.

I did end up using an on-call room. Thankfully, it was empty and I got a few hours of sleep before I needed to get back up. I had full intentions of showering and being fresh for my favorite appointment. I put on fresh scrubs and tossed my hair up in a tasteful messy bun that Dawson liked so much. It was easy, and it was cute, and somewhat professional.

We had a trauma victim on their way in a few minutes before his appointment, and I let the receptionist know which room to take Dawson. Trip was off and available to bring him to see me. I sent him a quick text as I was waiting for the ambulance to arrive after the call came in, and let him know I might be a few minutes late, not knowing what I'd be dealing with.

Two doctors and I worked on the poor woman who had been severely beaten. She was covered in contusions, and took a horrible smack to the face, when she fell against a corner table. At least that's what the neighbor who came with her said.

There wasn't much I could do for her eyes until they got the internal bleeding under control. I helped where I could, and we worked on her swiftly until her blood pressure dropped unexpectedly, and she flatlined.

I wasn't expecting her to die.

We shocked her several times and tried a shot of epinephrine and nothing worked.

"Stand back, Doc," someone else in the room instructed. I was in complete shock at this turn of events.

"This wasn't her time," I whispered. I hadn't even had a chance to help her yet.

"At least we know she won't have to suffer anymore," a nurse said, as she was cleaning up the room. This wasn't the first time this woman had been battered and abused. And she wasn't my first patient to die. I wasn't sure why she gotten to me as hard as she had, but I was a mess.

"I have an appointment to get to," I told Selma, who was working the desk in the E.R. "And unless you need me, I'll grab lunch after."

"Sounds good, Doc," she said. "Chin up, O'Neale. You're an amazing doctor."

Her words were sincere and I needed to hear them, because I was currently down on myself, and not pleased with the outcome of the last patient. *At least she won't have to suffer anymore...*

I went into the exam room where Dawson and Trip were waiting, and closed the door behind me, heading straight to the sink to wash my hands again. It wasn't like me to carry my emotions from one patient to the next, but I didn't stop to take time to center myself and move on before coming in to see them.

"Hey, Vix," Dawson read my face immediately and knew I was not okay. "What happened?"

I scrubbed my hands longer than normal, and knew that Trip and Dawson were trying to figure out what to say to me, but there was nothing to say. I squeezed the edge of the counter and let out a big sigh, before turning to face them.

"Patient stuff," I said, and breathed in, trying to move on to the patient in front of me. "Hi."

"Hi," Dawson said back. He had already hopped up on the table and my hands were resting on his knees as I looked into his eyes, not because I was his doctor, just because I needed to see them and find comfort behind his ocean blues.

"How's the face today?" I asked, zoning back in to work.

"Not nearly as sore and I think I'm seeing better. At least, I did at bingo last night."

"That is great news," I told him. "Let's take care of these stitches first and then I'll get a good look at your eyes."

Trip watched every move I made and was a good assistant when I needed one. We got Dawson cleaned up and put a fresh bandage just to keep the salve that I put on his wound from getting in his eye. He wouldn't need to cover the cut any longer now that it was healing well.

"Do you normally do stuff other than ophthalmology?" Trip asked, as I was listening to Dawson. His heartbeat was soothing.

"Working in the E.R., I find I do more *other* things than I do eye stuff, oddly enough. Just depends on what patients need."

"That makes sense, you were a pro with those stitches,"

he said. I winked back at him and told Trip I was good with kids, teasing Dawson as if he wasn't in the room. He did well on his eye test and everything was looking good. He was healing well from the surgery, and I had high hopes he would get to the vision number he needed for his pilot's license to stay active.

"I haven't got a call that they need me back yet, so I have time for lunch if you guys would like to join me?"

"Are they serving pancakes?" Dawson asked, and looked over at Trip.

"For you, I bet we can make a special order."

CHAPTER THIRTY-EIGHT

"My make-up regime for work is pretty simple, if you couldn't tell," Vixie said. No, *I couldn't tell* other than the fact I knew she didn't spend hours getting ready in the morning. "So, I need to go get ready for the wedding at my place and pack for our road trip."

"You leaving me?" I didn't mean to sound like a child, but that was exactly how it came out.

"I thought maybe you'd want to come over and see my tiny apartment?"

"Why, yes, yes, I would. I'll bring my wedding clothes and we can get dressed at your place before heading to the beach." That was a solid plan.

"There's a little spot not too far from here where we could grab brunch if you'd like? Or take something back to my place? I have nothing there to cook," she said with a giggle. "Grocery day has long-since passed since I met you, and it doesn't sound like it'll be coming back around for a little while, anyway."

"Brunch date. I like it." I'd order pancakes. *Again.* Because they were my favorite.

The booth we got was small, but intimate, in that I could sit near her and sneak and rub my fingers up and down her thigh. After we ordered, I put my arm around her, and she settled in next to me.

We fit together nicely.

They brought her mocha iced coffee and boasted free refills, which I thought was cool, and apparently, was her favorite thing about the place. *Figures.* Vixie wasn't a big eater. She got a half-size biscuit and gravy with one egg over easy. I could have swallowed that in three bites. My big breakfast came and I was glad she nibbled a little bit on my pancakes. It felt good sharing things with her and seeing her smile.

"So, your parents live here in Boca right?" I asked, not sure where they ended up settling after she said her father had retired.

"They do. They have a penthouse condo on the beach not too far from here. It was a midlife-crisis purchase for my mother. She was tired of housekeeping and liked the idea of the view."

"Can't say I blame her there, I enjoy not having to pick up after myself too." I pushed my food around my plate, afraid to ask the next question, but after a big gulp of pineapple juice, I decided, why not? "Have you told your parents about me?"

"*Ha!*" She practically snorted. "No, not yet. My mother would already be planning our children's sweet-sixteen parties if that was the case."

"Oh, Mom likes to be involved, got it." My eyes got big and I tried to hide any kind of reaction.

"She means well, and she really does want me to settle down, but it's just not been time yet. Hadn't met the right fella."

"I understand how that goes. I've been flying free for a while now and trying to enjoy every minute." I took another drink of juice. "I will admit it has been nice settling here for the past week, feeling like I have a place to come home to, even if it's Trip's old condo."

"Do you ever go back to your dad's place?" she asked. I hadn't gotten into the major details of that, but when my father moved into the retirement community, we sold everything to pay for his new place.

"There's not a place to go back to anymore," I admitted. "We sold the family farm to Aunt Faye when my father started showing signs of dementia, and made her the executor of his accounts, since I wasn't as easily reached." I explained to Vixie that Griffin Manor was a retirement community with several layers of care for Spring City's aging residents. Those who were self-sufficient, had condos that surrounded the larger buildings that housed residents needing more assisted-living options.

"That must feel... well, different, I guess... not having a place to call home?"

"I definitely feel like the town is my home, and I can visit my aunt any time I want, but yeah... no real place to hang my hat. It didn't make a whole lot of sense for me to get an apartment to just let it sit empty most of the time."

"Well, I understand that. Mine is empty a whole lot more than I'm there." It became more apparent that we led similar, but different lives, the two of us. "Where did you say the wedding is taking place?"

"A resort... lemme check my phone, I have the details." I was horrible at remembering stuff like that, so I appreciated the email they sent with all the details. "It's at the Classico... the information says we're supposed to arrive between 7:10 and 7:25."

"Coulda guessed that was the place..." Vixie pushed her plate away from her. She had been done for a while, and I was slower than Christmas finishing my food.

"Yeah? They do a lot of weddings there?"

"Yep, all the time. Lots of people come to Florida to get married."

"Makes sense, I suppose... the whole getaway thing." I didn't mind the idea.

"You might just get to meet my parents after all."

"What makes you say that? Are we planning a visit?" I was trying to hurry at this point so it wouldn't feel like she was waiting on me.

"No, that's just where they live..." she slurped the last sip of coffee, "...so we could totally run into them."

Ohh.

CHAPTER THIRTY-NINE

I didn't want to scare him off, but my father often came and went at all hours of the day, and my mother liked walking on the beach in the evening. It was totally possible we'd run into them. And if I didn't say something to my mother about attending a wedding at her place, she'd know something was up, *AND THEN* she'd want to know about my date, and who he was, and why I hadn't mentioned him, and I suddenly wanted to barf.

Dawson's phone rang as we headed to my apartment.

"It's Trip," he said. "Hey man, what's up?"

He put him on speaker phone, so I could say hello and listen too.

"So, I called around and found the business that backs up to the pond across from the condo, and talked to their manager."

"Okay? Not sure where you're going with this, but I'm all ears," Dawson said. I wasn't sure either.

"They have a camera that has a clear view of the back-side of the condo, and he let me look at the footage from last night."

"Oh really, did you see anything?"

"It's not zoomed in enough to make out faces, but I can see the body types of the people, and have an idea. I don't want to put thoughts in your head until you see the photos yourself, so I'll bring them with me tonight to the wedding, and we can talk it out over a few beers."

"Sounds good, I don't like that you're being cryptic, but it sounds like you made a little headway."

"I think so too. I gotta go get Brucey and take him over to the resort... he's the flower guy, or whatever they call it."

"Ring bearer, Trip. He's the ring bearer." I couldn't help myself.

"Yeah, that's it. I'll see you guys in a couple hours."

Dawson hung up and I could see he was contemplating as I drove.

"Any idea what Trip is thinking?"

"No, and that's what concerns me. He thinks I'll recognize them, so that means whoever it was knew I was there, and wasn't just breaking into the place looking to burglarize."

I hadn't thought about it like that. I left him to his thoughts as we made it to my apartment.

"Home sweet home," I said, and let him into my one-bedroom studio. The one thing going for the place was the openness, and that I was able to have my big comfortable bed. It was the main reason I had an apartment, to sleep in peace, and that was exactly what I did when I crashed.

"This is adorable, Vix. It's so you."

"Thanks! Make yourself comfortable. I'll go pack and get that over with," I said. "How long are we planning on being gone?"

"Uhhh, hadn't really thought that far ahead?" *I didn't figure he had.*

"'kay, I can pack accordingly." I was easygoing enough. I'd toss in a few outfits that could work for whatever and be good to go. I didn't plan on spending time with Dawson and his father, rather I'd chauffeur him there and give him some space.

"Oh, speaking of that, I should get us a room." I tried not to laugh. He was not a planner when it came to this kind of stuff. I could tell he really did fly by the seat of his pants when he was on layovers.

"I figure we can get up early and head north? It'll be a long day of driving, so if you'd rather stop halfway, we can?"

"Sounds good to me. I think I'll be okay to drive some, if you trust me, that is... and if you'd rather we can get a rental, instead of putting miles on your Tahoe?"

"Nah, I don't mind. Just got the oil changed a few weeks ago too, so she's good to go."

"Are you gonna have any more eye games for me to play on the road trip?"

I hadn't thought about it, but I should have come up with something to keep him working on his eyesight.

"I'll guess you'll have to wait and *see*..." Pun was totally intended.

"I can't wait to *see*..."

I did my makeup, and tossed things in my suitcase, while he hung out on the bed flipping channels. We lounged around until it was time to get ready to head over to the resort.

The rusty rose-colored high/low wrap dress I got from the boutique Kisha recommended was open just enough to be sexy in all the right places, without going overboard, or being slutty. I loved the cap sleeves and low v-neck, so I could get away not wearing a bra. The panty line was my biggest concern.

167

"Be honest, can you see a line?" Dawson was just going to have to tell me.

"Holy mother, what line might I be looking for? You're fucking gorgeous." I thought I blushed a little, but held it together.

"Right here, is there a line?" I pointed at my rear.

"Come closer," he said, sitting on the edge of my bed. "I don't see too well, so I need a better look."

"You see fine!" I snorted! He was teasing. "Like, come on now, this is serious. If I need to wear a thong, I will, but I don't want to on the off chance it gets windy and catches my dress."

"No, we do not want that," he said, and ran his hand up my leg, sliding his fingers under the aforementioned panty line. "I can't see... this... through your dress. But, unless you want these on the floor, you're gonna need to let *me* finish getting ready."

"Later, love. *Later*."

CHAPTER FORTY

The resort was nothing short of magnificent. After looking up and seeing the penthouse from the ground, I didn't blame Mrs. O. one bit for wanting to move in.

We arrived on time and I wore my sunglasses. The ceremony caught the sunset and the atmosphere was really nice.

I managed to snag a handhold during the ceremony, which tickled me. I hadn't been on a *real* date in ages.

"Congratulations Captain and Mrs. McCormack," I said, as we approached the bride and groom. I'd like to introduce my... uh..." I stalled for a second, but didn't look at Vixie. I was gonna wing it, "...my girlfriend, Dr. Vixie O'Neale."

"Everett, please call me Everett, and this is my beautiful bride, Grace," he said, and they shook hands.

"Beautiful ceremony. Thank you for having me," she said, with manners and class. I wondered if she ended up telling her mother about being at the resort for the wedding. I needed to remember to ask later.

"Please, enjoy the evening," Grace said, and we went inside to find our table and grab drinks. I was pleased to find Trip and Kendall along with two other couples from the airline were at our table. Brucey was swooning the flower girl in the kids' section.

As more guests came in, they dimmed the lights, which made me relieved. I was tired of squinting and didn't want Vixie to notice and make me put my sunglasses on inside.

Since I hadn't RSVP'd properly, Vix and I ended up with the chicken, which was default for those who hadn't picked what kind of meat they wanted. I was slightly jealous of Trip's steak, even though it looked a little too done for me. Once the dances started and things were less formal at our table, I scooted over, so he could show me the pictures from the surveillance camera.

"Vixie! Let's go dance!" Kendall said, and came over and stole my date.

"Okay!" she said with a WOO, and they took the other ladies from the table as well. The guys excused themselves to go find more drinks, and Trip and I had a little privacy to look at his discovery.

"No way," I couldn't contain myself.

"I figured you'd recognize them, even with a bad eye," Trip said.

"Why were they... what on earth? What do they want?" I could not get the words out to save my life.

"I dunno. Seems pretty fishy to me. But, I want to investigate this a little further."

"Oh, man, I forgot to tell you. Well, I didn't forget, it just kinda happened fast, and today's really the first time I've seen you to tell you." I explained that Aunt Faye had called and Vixie was going to take me to Kentucky to see my dad.

"Fuck, man. I hope he's alright. And Vixie. Shit, you got a good one there. I dare say she might actually like you back." Trip always had a way with words.

"Yeah, I hope so too, and I kinda think she might like me a little."

"What exactly is gonna happen with that when you get back in the cockpit?" He was saying what I had been thinking for a while.

"That's been on my mind too. We keep dancing around that conversation." Dancing. I could see her out on the dance floor with Kendall and the others, and either I was wearing rose-colored glasses, or she was easily the most beautiful girl in the room. The songs faded and they came back to the table.

"I'm gonna get a fresh drink," Vixie said, and kissed my cheek before excusing herself. She nodded that she'd grab one for Kendall too as Trip's bride took her seat beside him.

"I'll make you some road-tripping playlists tonight to help pass the time."

"Aw, that's a great idea. You know I enjoy a good playlist."

They announced the first dance with the bride and groom, and then the expected dances with the father of the bride and the mother of the groom. Vixie sat beside me, obviously freshened up from the ladies' room, and snuggled up to my side. Fuck, it felt good to have her near me.

Vixie leaned in, and whispered in my ear, "Is the Commander going to ask me to dance, or is he going to make me sit back, and watch the rest of the evening?" Her breath on my ear gave me goosebumps, and hearing her call me *Commander* was hella sexy. How could I say no to that?

"Would you like to dance?" I asked, and reached out my hand for hers.

Holding her tight against me as we swayed back and forth to love songs was the most perfect part of the evening. For a few minutes we were able to tune everybody else out and it felt like only the two of us were in the room.

"This dress really is gorgeous," I told her, as we danced. "I can't wait to check out your panty line later."

"Nooo," she pulled her head off my shoulder. "You said you couldn't see it!"

"I can't with your dress on!" I whispered with gusto. "But later, this pretty little dress will be on the floor!"

She managed a smirk, and we went back to swaying, until the DJ announced it was cake time.

"We'll talk more later," Trip said to me, as we all headed across the dance floor with the rest of the crowd. "I plan on paying the bar where we had Everett's bachelor party a little visit..." he said, "...and I'll be inquiring about Diamond and Bruno, by name, and why they broke into your condo."

"Can't wait to hear how that goes!"

CHAPTER FORTY-ONE

We got up at 5 a.m. to get ready and head north to Kentucky. It wasn't much earlier than I got up for a normal day at the hospital, so I didn't complain too much.

Even though the reason for the trip wasn't necessarily the most positive, I was excited to be getting out of Dodge for a while. I realized I hadn't had a real vacation since I was in college. And while this trip didn't have any tourist stops planned, it was still a getaway, and I was enjoying the heck out of the company.

"So, my only concessions are when we see a good place for coffee and/or ice cream, we have to stop." It was 5:23 a.m., and those were my instructions as we hit the open road.

"Oh dear, this trip could take days," Dawson said, and put his sunglasses on. In the dark. Just to ignore me.

"Rest your eyes, playboy. I'mma make you drive later." *Well, as long as he was comfortable.*

I grabbed us each soda from the fridge before we departed, so that caffeine was enough to keep me awake and cruising. Dawson was quiet for a while as we rode in silence. As the sun came up, he pulled down his visor to block the rays. I wasn't sure if that was to appease me, or because it was bothering him. I also didn't want to put on my doctor hat and ask.

"Breakfast options. You want to grab something to eat in the car, or stop somewhere and eat inside?"

"I'd be good with a chicken biscuit, so we can keep putting miles behind us, you?"

"You know what I'm after, so that sounds just fine."

Big coffee, check.

Chicken biscuit, check.

On the road again, check.

"Oh yeah, Trip made us a playlist. Complete with notes for each track..." Dawson held up the folded yellow piece of paper. Without taking my eyes off the road for more than a second, I could see that track one said "Just kidding" next to it.

"Oh, I can't wait for this!"

Dawson connected his phone to my Bluetooth in the Tahoe and pulled up the *Road TRIPpin' Playlist.*

Track one was some sort of medieval song that made us look at each other and laugh. Probably exactly what Trip was going for.

"Onto the next," he said.

Track two... Road Trippin' by the Red Hot Chili Peppers.

"Much better," I said. We ate and listened. As the miles went by, I could tell something was on Dawson's mind. "Whatcha thinkin' about?"

"My dad," he said softly.

"Want to talk about it?"

"I dunno. I guess I'm feeling guilty for all the time that's passed that I have been away. Not that he would have known who I was for most of it, but just my lack of being around."

"It's in the past, Dawx. Can't change it, you can only

move forward." I was kind of proud of that off-the-cuff advice.

"My dad taught me how to fly. We did crop dusting in a small plane for years as I was growing up. When I got to my teens, I wanted to learn how to fly other planes, so by high school he made that happen for me. I had flight hours well before college and made it through my bachelor's degree faster than most," he paused. "Then, I kinda flew away. When things started going downhill for him, Aunt Faye stepped in, and I came back only a handful of times. I just wanted to fly away. Not look back... and here I am looking back."

"Where exactly does your Aunt Faye live?" I asked.

"She lives on a big farm that's been in our family for generations. When Dad moved into the retirement community, Faye bought out my parents' portion of the land to pay his bills and has been renting out the farmhouse where I grew up."

"That's good that it stayed in the family."

"Yeah, I'm glad she was able to do that at the time. I know Dad was too. He was still himself then, but had been diagnosed as he was starting to forget things," he said. Dawson picked at his fingernails, and I could tell talking about this was hard for him.

"You have made one heck of a career for yourself, Dawson. Your parents would be proud of you."

"Yeah, I know... it'll be weird being home too. Haven't been back for years."

"Where are we staying? I meant to ask."

"There's a bed and breakfast in town where everybody stays. It's really nice. I think you'll like it. A little coffee shop right down the street too."

"He knows the way to my heart," I teased.

"No hospital bed either... that gonna be a problem?"

"I think we can manage," I winked. "We can prop you up a little, so you're elevated, but you should be fine."

He reached over and laid his arm on my leg, rubbing my knee as we drove.

"Looking forward to sleeping in a real bed?"

"Looking forward to sleeping in a real bed *with you*," he said.

CHAPTER FORTY-TWO

The trip took almost fifteen hours to make it to the bed and breakfast in Spring City. We stopped for bathroom breaks and to grab food and snacks and kept on driving. I drove for about an hour and then stopped at a rest area to let Vixie take back over. I was seeing okay, but caught myself squinting, and didn't want to put us at risk.

We had an amazing night together.

Once visiting hours were open at the retirement community the next morning, we grabbed a coffee, and headed over to see my dad. I let Aunt Faye know I was in town the night before and that we'd likely see her for lunch.

"Oh, there's a nice gazebo... I can sit there and read while you visit with your father," Vixie told me, as we parked at the retirement community.

"You're... not going in with me?"

"I, uh, I honestly didn't figure you'd want me to. I don't want to impose, but I'll do whatever you want me to do," she said. I got the feeling she didn't want to be another stranger, especially not knowing how he would react.

"Let's both go in and see how he's doing... if you don't mind? Can always split up later?"

"I don't mind at all," she said, and took my hand as we went inside. He had been moved to the highest level of care since I had last visited, and the area felt more like a hospital than the other sections.

We stopped to see the nurse before going in.

"Hello, Dawson," Nurse Kitty Brawand said, as I walked up. "Good to see you, son."

"My, my, Nurse Brawand, it's been a long time, how are you?" I recognized her immediately. I was friends with her son growing up and we played little league together.

"Your daddy is a changed man... since the last time you saw him... just want you to be prepared for that," she said.

"I talked with Faye, but I'm not exactly sure what the prognosis is, or what's going on?" I wanted to ask how much longer he had, but *didn't* at the same time.

"He has Huntington's Disease, you knew that right?" she said.

"Yes, I've heard that term, but not in several years as his dementia had become more of the problem."

"Right, well, Huntington's has caused the progression of dementia. He's not going to get better, Dawson... but I think you knew that."

"Yeah," I said softly. "I knew that."

"What he's experiencing now is a huge loss of everything in different stages. He has trouble eating by himself, going to the bathroom without assistance, walking, talking, and sadly, remembering. For patients experiencing this, they can get angry, because they want to be able to do things on their own," she explained. "But they just can't get their brain to execute the actions, and this causes frustration."

Vixie nodded her head as Kitty talked. I knew she was understanding what was going on better than me.

"What can we do for him?" I asked.

"Just being there when you can. Sometimes he's lucid. We had a nice conversation the other day about you and Jamal, and the little league championship y'all won. He remembered it like it was yesterday, and a few minutes later, didn't even know who I was. So, he's in there, and when he's able to come out, he does."

"Can I go visit for a bit?" I asked Kitty.

"Absolutely, but first you have to introduce me to your friend," she said with a smile.

"Oh, I am so sorry, where are my manners? Nurse Kitty Brawand this is my girlfriend, Dr. Vixie O'Neale."

"You got yourself a doctor? Shew wee, Dawson! And she's a looker too!" They smiled at each other and Vixie blushed, but didn't say much. We still hadn't talked about the use of the term girlfriend, but at this stage in the game I didn't know what else to call her. A conversation for later, I assumed.

She pushed open the door slowly and quietly, as I figured she did with other patients' room doors too, so as to not startle them.

"Mr. K.? You have a visitor," she said, and we snuck in behind her. My father was lying on a hospital bed, wearing a brown robe, pajamas and slippers. He appeared to be watching The Price is Right.

"Hey, there," I said, and went over to sit next to him.

"Mr. K., this is Dawson and Vixie. They wanted to come in and watch a little TV with you, if that's okay?" Kitty asked, trying to feel out how he was doing.

"Sure, I've got two chairs, they can watch TV with me."

I sat next to him and Vix sat on the other side. She

seemed more comfortable than me and for that I was a little jealous. I guessed she was used to seeing patients all the time and my father felt like a stranger to me.

"I'll be right out here if you need anything, Mr. K.," Kitty said, and left the door half open as she went back to the nurses' station.

"This show was so much better when Bob Barker was the host," he said.

"I totally agree. I used to watch it with my dad when I was growing up. Plinko was my favorite game."

"Of course, it's everyone's favorite." *Not the first time he had said that.*

"So, how do you like this place? It's my first time visiting here," Vixie said, after a few minutes of silence. She knew I didn't know what to say or do.

"Eh, food's crap. Sometimes I get a cute nurse. And sometimes I get to go outside."

"You like going outside?" I asked.

"Yep, sometimes I'll see a plane overhead. I like to hear them fly by." His words caught me off guard and I didn't realize that little piece of enjoyment would fill me with such sadness. Vixie looked over at me and saw me trying to keep it together.

"I love planes too!" she said. "You know what's neat? Dawson here is a pilot!"

"You are? I used to be a pilot," he said, not taking his eyes away from the TV. "My son is a pilot too. Flies big planes. I used to fly an old crop duster... he's in the big time."

"I fly the big ones too," I said. "Usually Boeing 747, and some smaller Boeings around the U.S. I fly even bigger planes when I'm piloting international flights."

"How many passengers does a 747 hold? 350?"

"Pretty close... how many passengers does a crop duster hold?"

"Ha! Just one!" I got him tickled and it was good to hear my old man laugh. "How have you been, son?"

And just like that, he was my father again.

"Doing good, Dad. They treating you okay here?"

"Yep, they are. Kitty makes sure. Come give your old man a hug," he said. And I did. I hugged his neck hard and he hugged me back.

"Sorry it's been so long." I didn't know what to say.

"It's alright, Dawson. You've got to live your life, son." He looked over to Vixie. "And who is this pretty girl?"

"Dad, this is Vixie. She's my girlfriend."

"He being good to you, sweetheart?" he asked.

"Very good, sir, it's a pleasure to meet you," she said, and reached out her hand to hold his.

"I know our time is fleeting. I'm rarely myself these days. But there's one thing I want to tell you, Dawson. And that's how I want you to find somebody that will make you happy. Happy like your mama made me. You deserve all the love in the world, kiddo. Even though she was taken from me too soon, I wish for you the kind of love we had."

"Thanks, Pop. I know what you and Mom had was something special."

"Are you a doctor?" he asked Vix. "I heard somebody say Doctor O'Neale. Is that my new doctor?"

"I am a doctor, sir. But I'm just visiting here with Dawson. I'm not *your* doctor."

"Can't find a good doctor around here." The inflection in his voice was changing as he spoke. "Damn show was better when Bob Barker was the host."

And just like that, he was gone again.

"The one who has never sat on plane think being on plane is a mesmerising experience, the one who sit frequently thinks flying the plane would be a mesmerising thing. The one who fly all day craves to sleep peacefully on land. Got the point?"

- Sarvesh Jain

CHAPTER FORTY-THREE

It took a lot of strength for me to hold it together for Dawson. I saw patients all the time go through memory loss, and families dealing with the effects, but seeing this strong man break down with his father broke my heart.

Dawson showed me around Kentucky like a first-class tourist. We spent time with his dad in the mornings before going on adventures to Churchill Downs, The Louisville Slugger Museum and The Kentucky Horse Park. There was a cute little ice-cream place in town that we stopped at twice too. Their signature flavors were Birthday Cake and S(mint)ten Chocolate Chip from a place called Frost Ice Cream Company. I was so impressed, I made a note to look them up, and see if there were any locations in Florida that carried the brand. The local coffeehouse also was exceptional. I wanted to bottle them up and take them with me.

On our way south, he wanted to stop and do a tour of Mammoth Cave, so we did that too. I hadn't realized I was actually claustrophobic until we were squeezing in between rocks. The whole experience was beautiful.

"I'm not back on the clock until Sunday," I told him, as

we drove down the interstate back home. "Anywhere else you want to stop on the way?"

"Really? You're not tired of me yet?" he teased.

"Not yet... I do want to check your eye soon though, and see how well you're seeing. It's been about two weeks, right?"

"Yep. Time sure flies."

I knew he was anxious to get back in a plane, but I thought he was also nervous about the inevitable, and didn't want to know how well his sight had improved.

"Even if you're not back down to your old better-than-20/20 self, that doesn't mean you won't meet the requirements to fly," I tried to reassure him.

"I know, I know. It's just been a lot to take in, I guess."

"Are you feeling better about your dad since our visit?" I asked.

"Yeah. Still feeling a little guilty for being away so much, but I'm planning to remedy that and spend more layovers at Faye's, so I can see Dad more often. I can fly into Lexington or Louisville easily and crash for a long weekend as I have time."

The windows were cracked open and my hair was wafting in the breeze as we chatted. My cell phone buzzed in my pocket. It must have just been a text message because it stopped. *Probably my mother.*

"I'd like to go to the beach or pool or something, before you have to get back to work, how does that sound?"

"Sounds great. I never get enough beach time anymore and I would like that. Maybe I'll take you over to my parents and we can hang out at their pool..."

"Ohhh, meet the parents...? I'm moving up in the world. Your mom will start naming our grandchildren!" I swatted at him.

"She very well might!" I said. "I did meet your dad after all, I wouldn't mind returning the favor if you want to meet my overprotective, pushy parents."

"I'll be a gentleman," he said. The thought of him being anything else made me smile. He always was a gentleman.

This time his phone rang.

"Hey, man," Dawson said, and put his phone on speaker.

"Hey y'all, how's the road trip?"

Trip and Dawx talked for a few minutes about showing me around Kentucky before he said he had news.

"I went to the bar where we had Everett's bachelor thing," Trip said. "Talked to the bartender. Bruno and Diamond weren't there at the time, but are regulars and had been running their mouths about *the hot-shot pilot* that Bruno slugged, and he planned on suing for kicks."

"You've got to be kidding me," Dawson said. An audible *no* escaped my lips, and I stayed focused on the road.

"I wish I was kidding. From what I can gather, they were looking for your information... likely your social security number and full name. The bartender said that Bruno and some other guys got into another fight later that night, and Bruno plans to pin the assault on you. Figured you had money, because you're a pilot."

"The bartender told you this? And would he be willing to make a statement to the police telling them the same thing?" Dawson's cheeks were getting redder by the second.

"Before you blow a gasket. Let me tell you the rest," Trip had time to calm down, which Dawson had not and was just getting going. "I took the pictures from the security camera to the officer who came out the night of the break-in. He said they weren't good enough quality to ID anyone, and that he'd made a note as to what the bartender had told me.

He had someone check and no suit has been filed against you."

"Well, that's good at least."

"He also said we should have called the fight in and got it on record when it happened." *Yes, you should have.*

"So what do we do?"

"Unfortunately, we just wait. I think you need to make sure your identity doesn't get stolen too, since your social security number may have been lifted from your medical paperwork," Trip was wise and I would follow his advice and put some safeguards in place.

"And is the condo okay?" Dawson asked.

"Yep and while you were gone I asked management to have new locks installed on the back sliding glass door and window alarms. Can't do much with the front door, as management has to be able to change that lock code as staff changes."

"Staff. Changes." I could have sworn I saw a lightbulb go off over Dawson's head.

"Yeah, like at hotels, you know, when they have new cleaning people, they change the locks."

"Oh, I've gotcha. And I think I may have just figured out how to deal with old Bruno."

CHAPTER FORTY-FOUR

"Hey, Mom."

Vixie had just gotten through saying she had to make a phone call before her mother freaked out for her lack of response. It made me think about my own life, and how I thought it was nice sometimes not to have anyone to report to.

"Road trip is ending a day early... yeah, we just decided to head home... mind if we come by tomorrow to swim...? Thinking a beach day sounds nice... okay... see you tomorrow... love you too." And that was that.

"Sounds like that worked out?"

"Yep, just gotta watch that eye of yours."

"Sure will, Doc. I'm gonna need some swim trunks though... can we go shopping?"

"You don't have any trunks?" *Why was that a surprise?*

"I've told you... everything I have has to fit in my suitcases, so when I get new things, old things have to go. I got rid of the trunks the last time I bought a new pack of T-shirts." Gotta make room, after all.

"You do look good in a white T-shirt." I said. "As long as

you don't get rid of your grey sweatpants to make room for your new trunks, I guess I understand."

I did not understand.

"You like my sweatpants?"

"Mmm hmm."

Well, okay then.

"Looks like we're about four hours from Boca... wanna grab some dinner? And then finish the trip?"

"Sounds fantastic, I'm starving!" I was always hungry. I could eat any time of the day. Guess that was due to my weird meal times coinciding with flights.

"There's this place in Ocala I've been wanting to try. If they have outdoor seating available, I'd say we're dressed nicely enough," she said.

"You're taking me to a fancy place?

"Steaks okay?"

I was not ever going to argue with a steak.

We didn't have to wait long and she called it on the outdoor seating. It was a good choice.

"I know this is gonna make me sound like a girl, but we're kind of on a date. Like a real date." Her giggle always made me smile.

"Yes, this is kind of like a real date. As opposed to all the other things we've been doing for the last two weeks," she said and shrugged her shoulders.

We had a nice dinner, and only had one glass of wine apiece, since we still had a ways to drive before we made it back to Boca.

"Let's run in this department store just down the street real quick and grab you some trunks," Vixie said, as we headed to the car. I was down for that. Would save time before going to her parents.

I picked up a couple pairs and started to go to the checkout when she stopped me.

"You're not going to try them on?"

I looked at the trunks in my hand and they were my size and looked like they would fit, so no, I was not.

"Nah, they'll be fine." They would, I was confident.

"What if they don't fit?" She was serious. I wasn't sure why, but the look on her face was telling me to go try them on.

"They'll fit." It was a dude thing. We knew when clothes would fit.

"But what if they don't?"

"Then I guess I'll donate a new pair of trunks and find something else tomorrow? Perhaps I could swim in grey sweatpants?"

"Boys really are different from girls," she said. It was fun getting to know how her mind worked and the little intricacies that you only found out about a person when you were dating.

"Ohh, I might need some sunscreen too... definitely none of that in my suitcase."

"I gotcha covered on sunscreen, you can borrow some of mine," she said.

"You promise to apply it properly? Don't want any weird tan lines, capisce?"

"I will do my best..."

"Let's get some ice cream and hit the road, shall we?" It got her mind off my trunks not fitting.

We made small talk on the last leg of the trip, and I thought we were both happy to see the sign for Boca. It felt good getting back to Silver Shores. I needed to do some laundry after our trip, and the condo had started feeling like it was home base. *Home* was a word I hadn't used in a while.

"I brought my bikini in case we swam on our trip, so we can just go from here tomorrow. My parents have plenty of towels and stuff at their place."

"I noticed you didn't tell your mom who you were bringing with you when you talked to her earlier..."

"You're just gonna be a surprise. Please, let's just not tell her you're a patient. Not a conversation I want to have with her, or my father..."

"My lips are sealed."

I noticed her phone buzzing again.

And she ignored it again.

"Sure I'm not keeping you from something?" I asked.

"Nope. Not. At. All."

CHAPTER FORTY-FIVE

It had never crossed my mind that my mother would invite guests on a random Saturday that I planned to come over and swim.

But yet, she had.

I wouldn't have cared, but when I saw Denny, I knew what she was up to and that Zak had to be there too. I had ignored his texts for the last few days, and didn't even read them to see what they said. Had I opened them, I'd have found out they would be coming by for a beach day, just like I planned for me and Dawson.

"Hey, Mom," I said, with less enthusiasm than usual. "You didn't tell me you invited guests."

"Well, dear, you didn't give me much time to tell you yesterday when we spoke." She looked behind me, practically having to pick her chin up at the sight of Dawson. "Now don't be rude, dear, introduce me to your friend."

"Mom, this is Dawson Kaczmarek... Dawx, this is my mom, Vickie O'Neale," I said. The swooner reached out his hand to take hers and kiss her knuckle. *You get points for that one, Dawson.*

"So, uh, who all is here?"

"Denny and his friend Zak are out at the pool. Thought it would be fun, since they said they wanted to have a beach day the last time y'all were together." *Great, Ma. Great.*

I didn't even know what Dawson and I were doing. We were having a good time, a fling—hell I didn't know what to call it, but I had no idea how things were going to play out or work out after he got back to work. So, this was bound to be awkward.

"There's stuff on the bar outside to make mimosas, enjoy yourselves," my mother said, as she went into the library. It didn't appear my dad was home and I was thankful we didn't have to talk to her.

"If this is weird, you can have some family time and I'll grab an Uber," Dawson said, pointing over his shoulder at the door. Yeah, it was weird, but he was the last person I wanted to go.

"Nope. Swimming. Mimosas. Relaxing. Today is going to be good." I just didn't know how I was supposed to act around Zak. But I was about to find out. We exited the penthouse onto the terrace where there was an outside bar, fancy landscaping and the rooftop pool. Mom had pulled out the screens so the sun wasn't so direct and there were shade areas. It was another reason I thought it would be a good place to swim with Dawx. *Shade and privacy.* So much for privacy.

"There's my favorite cousin," Denny came over and hugged me, as usual. "And she brought a friend."

"Sup man," Dawson said, and shook his hand.

"Denny. This is my buddy, Zak. Nice to meet ya." I slid over to the bar to kick back a mimosa and ignore the boys.

"Make yourself at home, Dawx," I said. Zak bypassed

Dawson as I figured he would and came over to where I was standing at the bar. "Hey, Zak."

"Wasn't sure if you were going to show... you didn't respond to my texts." *Fuck, could he be any louder about it?*

"I have had a busy week! Mimosa?" He shook his head. He and Denny had already settled outside and were only wearing their swim trunks. When Dawson pulled his crisp white T-shirt over his head, his brand new trunks slid a little farther down his waist and caught in his hip bones. My word, I caught myself drooling.

"Actually, yeah, I'd like a mimosa. Is that pineapple juice?"

"Huh? Um. Yeah. Yeah, mom knows I like mine made with pineapple juice, but there's orange juice here too." Sorry Zak, I was distracted by Dawson's flawless V and tan body I had only seen in dim lighting up until now. Fuck me. Speaking of, *that* was a fine idea.

"Pineapple juice sounds good," Zak said, and moseyed in front of my view, so I'd pay attention to him. That was when Dawson turned around and I got a clear view of his shoulders and the tattoo I couldn't make out when he was lying in the hospital bed. They were wings spread across his shoulder. The word "mom" was intricately woven throughout the feathers. How had I not noticed this before? I was having to cock my head around Zak to get a clear view, when I realized he was talking to me.

"Here you go, want to take one to Denny too?" That was more of an order than a request. I didn't know what to do about Zak, but I knew right here, right now, Dawson was the only one I wanted to give any of my attention.

"Come get in the pool, Vix... the water is great!" Denny was already in the water and Zak headed back over to their chairs. I scooted two other chairs back a little, so they were under the shade, convenient enough to be easier on Dawson's eye, and to get us farther away from the others.

"So sunscreen, you promised?" Dawson said. "I'll get your back if you get mine."

"I'll get your back... and your front... and your sides... and anywhere else you want, handsome." He had me all hot and bothered with his striptease.

"Ohhh, I like that offer, maybe later? I've never been one to show off," he said, and nodded in Denny's direction. The spray lotion was easy to apply, sadly, so there wasn't much work to be done on my part. Rubbing the lotion in on his shoulders, I wanted to ask about the tattoo.

"I like your wings," I said, not knowing what else to say.

"They're special to me, that's for sure." On so many levels, I understood this and loved him a little more knowing why.

I went to sit my stuff on the chair and slid my sundress over my head, noticing both Zak and Dawson enjoying the show.

This was awkward as hell.

"You want to swim for a little up here, or go down to the beach first?" I asked Dawson, out of earshot of the others.

"Walk on the beach later, maybe?"

"Okay, that sounds good. Promise me, you'll be extra careful about getting water in your eye. Don't make me play doctor here."

"Yes, ma'am," he said. "I won't take my sunglasses off and no going underwater."

"Grab your mimosa and your hat... let's go float for a little."

CHAPTER FORTY-SIX

"UK? As in University of Kentucky?" The guy named Zak said, nodding at my ballcap.

"Uh, yeah."

"You a fan of college basketball?" *Were we making small talk?*

Vixie grabbed a pool float shaped like a sloth and tossed it in the pool. I followed behind her and grabbed one shaped like a T-Rex.

"This one for me?" I asked, and couldn't help but smirk.

"Nope, that one's mine. It's my favorite. You can have the sloth." She was stinking cute climbing on her T-Rex float from the edge of the pool. "It's frigging cold, Denny! You liar!"

"Yeah, I like college basketball pretty well," I said to Zak, feeling bad I kind of ignored the guy for a minute.

"Yeah, me too. I'm a Duke fan though," he scrunched his face knowing my reaction. Two rival teams that did not, under any circumstances get along. Made sense why we had hit it off so well already.

"Sorry for your bad taste in teams, man."

"You gonna come master the sloth, or just stand there looking pretty?" Vix said from the pool. If I had been my old self, I'd have jumped in on her, but I refrained.

"I'm coming. You want another mimosa before I get in?" I knew she did.

"Oh, yes please. Spoil me!" I hadn't finished mine yet, so I topped it off and made her a fresh one before sliding them into the cup holders on her float.

"I'll hold yours until you get settled," she said.

"So, Dawson, how do you know my cousin?" Denny asked. He was settled on the corner steps of the pool with his own drink, and Zak was swimming around, getting too close to Vixie for my liking.

"I'm a pilot and we met a while back when I was on layover here in Boca." *Not a lie and vague enough to avoid how we really met.*

"That must be an awesome career, going anywhere in the world you want," he said.

"It has its ups and downs."

"Haha! You're funny!" Vixie chimed in. Her head was thrown back on the dinosaur, and she was fully enjoying her sunbathing experience.

"Where's home base for you, Dawson?"

"Uh, here in Boca mostly. I'm here more than most other places. My family is back in Kentucky." *Hence the hat, Zak.*

He was casually swimming around, like a shark in the water with my girl. I didn't like it one bit. This day was obviously a setup by Mrs. O. to get Zak and Vixie together. Had she told her about me, things might have gone differently. I just had to contain my jealousy and get along. I could do it, so long as he kept his distance.

Whatever he had done made her giggle, and the look from my direction made her instantly stop laughing, which was not my intention. *I liked her laugh.* I just didn't like him being the one to make her laugh.

She was cute lying on her favorite T-Rex floatie. I wanted to just gaze at her forever.

"So, Captain Dawson, where are you headed next? Is Captain how you address a pilot?" Denny asked.

"It—" Vixie cut me off.

"I prefer calling him Commander Kaczmarek. It has a ring to it, don't you think?"

"Frigging mouthful," Zak muttered under his breath.

"Captain—or Commander—either one is how you'd address a pilot. My friends call me Dawx." I looked over to Vix and she was smiling again. *Commander* had a nice ring to it when it rolled off her tongue.

"That nickname must have a story!" Denny was trying his damnedest to make conversation and I just did not want it.

"Indeed it does. A lot of drinking was involved, and a nickname was the result of that evening."

"No details? Pfft!"

"Maybe later after a few more drinks," I said.

"We have to pay attention for the little hot dog cart to come around," Denny said to Vixie.

"Yes, it's my favorite too," she looked over to me. "There's this little hot dog vendor that travels up and down the beach with this cart... if we're lucky, we'll catch him later and grab a hot dog."

"Boy that sounds like a rewarding career," Zak muttered.

Denny splashed water in their direction. "They're damn good hot dogs!"

"What do *you* do, Zak?" I was certain, based on his comment, he was not a hot dog vendor and was probably a doctor like the rest of them.

"I'm a cardiologist. Denny and I work in the same practice."

"Ahh, hearts are probably more rewarding than hot dogs, but I won't dis a man for making a living, especially one that makes him happy."

"Is flying a plane rewarding?" *Now the fucker was just pushing my buttons.*

"Actually it is. I've brought family members together, loved ones to see a sick relative before they passed away. I've flown soldiers home in pine boxes with a flag draped over top... People trust me with their lives, so yeah, it's rewarding."

And just like that I silenced the crowd.

Vixie stared at me through her big cat-eye sunglasses and I wished I knew what she was thinking.

"Ready to go stick your toes in the sand?" I asked. The pool area was entirely too hot-headed for my liking.

CHAPTER FORTY-SEVEN

Dawson was a trooper for putting up with Zak and Denny. I thought he realized when I first asked if he wanted to go down to the beach *before* the pool, why I was trying to get away from them, but alas, they decided to come with us. Mom and Dad's penthouse had four beach chairs that came with the place, so we didn't have to worry about finding a place to sit when we made it seaside. I brought a bag of towels and sunscreen... oh and cash for the hot dog cart, and we claimed the two chairs with the big umbrellas.

Denny and Zak could burn for all I cared.

I grabbed Dawson's hand and we headed out to get our feet wet. The eyes behind me were practically burning a hole through us as we strolled toward the water. But I didn't care. The sand in between my toes and my hand wrapped in his was perfect. If things didn't work out for me and Dawx, I didn't want to pursue anything beyond friendship with Zak.

"All the shell pickers have combed the beach already... they do every morning... but maybe we can find a pretty shell in the water," I said. "It's so clear today."

"It is, it's beautiful." He wasn't looking at the water. He

was looking at me.

We sloshed around and managed to get knee-deep without the waves getting too high. I hadn't seen any shells though as we puttered around in the water.

"Oh! Come here!" Dawson called me toward him. "There's a crab right by your foot... don't want you to step on it."

"A crab?! With pincers?" I freaked a little.

"They do live in the ocean, do they not?" Smart ass.

"Oh my God, OH MY GOD, it *is* under my feet!" I grabbed a hold of Dawson's winged shoulders and hoisted myself onto his back. "You're just gonna have to deal with it buddy. I did not like the feeling of that thing around my legs!"

"I gotcha, honey," he said, and very gentlemanly lifted me higher and held onto my legs, piggyback style. "Let's mosey over here away from the big sea creature."

"Ha ha ha, so funny... I'm sticking my tongue out at you, you just can't see it."

"I wish you'd put your arms around my neck a little tighter, I kinda like it," he said back. His jawline was so sharp from this angle and I couldn't get over how sexy he was in a ballcap and Ray-Bans.

I could see Denny and Zak coming our way from a distance. I'm sure they saw me freak out.

"What was it?" Denny asked. "You had to have seen something to panic like that!"

"Was it a shark?" Zak asked, as he came up behind Denny.

"No, it was not a shark!" I said in a loud whisper. "And don't say shark or we'll scare people!"

"It was a crab." Dawson said, very plainly, like it was no big deal.

"It's pincers grazed my ankle!"

Denny and Zak got a real big belly laugh at my expense.

"I think it's way over there now, if you're comfortable with me putting you down?" Dawson said to me, and let my legs slide down his backside.

"I'll walk you back to the beach, Vix, if you don't want to stay in the water."

"I'm good actually, just gonna swim a little." I looked over at Dawson. "Be right back."

I dove in head first and swam out a ways until it was too deep for me to touch the bottom. Just where I liked it. I had been swimming like a fish since I was a baby and I loved riding the waves. If I would have had more time as a teenager, I'd have tried surfing, but never wanted to make the commitment.

I could see the three of them in the water, but wasn't close enough to hear what they were saying, or if they were talking at all. I got my fill of the salt, just needing to swim a little and get it out of my system, and headed back to the boys.

"Dude, I'm *not* competition," I overheard Zak say, and saw him hold up his hands.

"No, you're not competition, because she's been in my bed every night for the past two weeks and not yours."

My jaw dropped as I came up behind them, Dawson was now walking away with his back to me while Denny and Zak were just standing there speechless. I don't think he saw me close enough to them that I would have overheard the last part of their conversation.

"Have fun with your *Commander*," Zak called out, as I passed him, and followed Dawson to the beach chair.

"Just... just shut the fuck up, Zak."

It was all I could muster.

"Without the pilot, there is no flying from one place to another."

- Lailah Gifty Akita

CHAPTER FORTY-EIGHT

I didn't realize Vixie was on my tail as I sat down on the beach chair, moving the umbrella so the shade was over my face. She sat down next to me and grabbed the towel out of her bag to dry off.

"Everything okay?" she asked. I wasn't sure what she had heard, but I wasn't talking about it.

"Yep, just getting a little headache. Too much sun. Not enough mimosas."

"We don't have to stay if you don't want to?" she said, trying to appease me. Truth was, I loved the beach. When I had layovers and time, it was the one place I wanted to go. I could lounge by myself, take in some sun, eat crappy beach food and drink girly drinks. What wasn't there to love? And now I had a new pair of trunks and would be prepared for the next time.

The next time.

Would the next time be here in Boca? Would the next time be here in Boca with Vixie? Or maybe just here in Boca with Trip, Kendall and Brucey. *Or maybe just by myself.* I had learned to be my best company.

"I'm gonna make your follow-up appointment on Monday, if that's okay?" she said. I knew we needed to do that and check to see how much progress had been made on my vision, but I was dreading it. The idea of me not being able to fly sank my soul, but I'd figure it out. If nothing else, maybe I would be in the range to still fly with correction. I had to hold onto that hope.

"That sounds good," I said, leaning my head against the back of the soft cushion. "I can get an Uber if Trip can't go with me."

I wasn't going to initiate the conversation before my appointment, but Vixie and I needed to have a talk about what was going to happen with us after I was healed up and back to normal. I understood why she'd want to keep her options open with Zak. He seemed like a nice enough guy, well *until he opened his mouth today*, but whatever. *I* wouldn't have picked him for her, but again, I could see why she would want to appear available.

"Vix, there's the hot dog stand!" Denny came running up beside her like a teenager. It was obvious they had been together since they were kids. It was priceless seeing the excitement on their faces as this fun thing from their childhood sprang up.

"Come on Dawx, you have to come make your dog... they have so many toppings!"

I could easily see why they liked the hot dog cart so much. It was cheap, easy, *tasty* and the guy had fresh lemonade shake-ups. I got a chili dog with onions and cheese and Vixie got what appeared to be a hot dog with everything but the kitchen sink. She topped it off with a big squeeze of mustard, which made me cringe a little.

"You don't like mustard?" she said, when she saw my face.

"No... and I'm wondering if I can love a girl who *does* like mustard."

"You... you loved me before I put mustard on my hot dog?" she said in disbelief. I didn't even really catch what I was saying when I said it either, but it felt like I did.

I shrugged my shoulders.

"Eat your nasty old mustard wiener," I said, and laughed. "Let's go sit back down."

The afternoon was quiet and I appreciated the fact that Denny and Zak pretty much left us alone. I didn't enjoy having to put him in his place, but I wasn't going to pretend that we were just acquaintances while he flirted with her all day long.

"Let's slip back up to the pool without our two tagalongs, whaddaya say?" Vixie asked softly so they wouldn't hear her. I nodded and we managed to get away without notice as they napped in the sun.

Vixie's mom had set out a tray of fruit and snacks for us, and continued to stay out of sight. I wondered when Vix would talk to her about me *and Zak,* and what she would say.

"Another mimosa? Or how about a beer?" she asked.

"That sounds great, actually." My head was still aching and I was happy to see the sun go behind the clouds for a little while. I knew the hat and sunglasses were helping, but I didn't want to sit in the shade any longer. I wanted to be in the pool with my girl.

I sat down on the side and stuck my feet in the water. It was cool, but a good temperature for the hot day. She brought two bottles over and set them down next to us, but instead of sticking her feet in, she hopped in and swam a couple laps, end to end. She really was a fish.

Vix came back over to me and slid her body in between my legs, resting her cold, wet arms on my thighs.

"Damn you're freezing!"

"And you sir, are hot! You might need some more sunscreen!"

"I'll be good for a little bit." I rubbed her arm and reached the other bottle of beer over so she could have a drink.

"I know you can fly, Commander, but can you swim too?" she asked, just curious I assumed, knowing that I wasn't going to risk getting chlorine in my eye.

"Yep. I swim too... maybe not as good as you, but I can hold my own."

Vixie sat the bottle down next to mine and continued to hang onto my legs, her feet unable to touch the bottom of the pool where she was floating.

"I'm glad your trunks fit." I knew she'd bring it up eventually when I didn't try them on at the store. "Since I saw you pull your shirt off earlier today and watched your trunks slide down and get caught on those sexy hips of yours, all I've wanted to do is to slide them down even further..."

"Want me to come in the water with you?" I asked, knowing the question had a lot more to it than simply getting in the pool.

"Yes, I do."

I got up from the side of the deep end and walked around to the shallow side where I could get in slowly at the steps. There was always that adjustment when you went from your skin being sun-kissed into the cool water. It took me a minute to get over to her, but I didn't want to go deeper than I could stand. I really *was* trying to be careful.

"Now what was it you were saying about my trunks?"

CHAPTER FORTY-NINE

Dawson waded over to me and I met him in the five-foot section of the pool, so we could both stand up.

"I said that I'd like those *trunks* better if they slid down your hips a little *farther*."

"Now hold on a second, my girl." His words, *my girl*, made butterflies in my belly. "I'm not gonna stop you, but you do realize we are in your parents' pool, and anybody could walk out here at any time, right? Including your cousin and the stuck-up cardiologist..."

"I fully acknowledge this statement and understand the potential consequences," I said, then I grabbed onto him, and wrapped my legs around his waist. The nice thing about the pool was the disguise of what was happening under the water. Unless you were in a helicopter, nobody would know what we were doing. My mother could look out from the window and it would look like we were just playing around.

I reached down and loosened the drawstring of his trunks, doing exactly what I had envisioned earlier in the day. I slid them down a little, finding out he was already ready for me.

"The strings on this cute polka dot bikini might be tied a little tight," he whispered in my ear. "I'm gonna loosen them a bit, 'kay?" *Hell if I was going to protest.*

It didn't take much effort for him to pull me close and slide inside. Face to face, my arms firmly around his neck, and we were at it again.

"You make me not want to do anything else but this," I whispered in his ear.

"Likewise. I wouldn't mind doing you forever."

<hr/>

"Staying at my place tonight? I know you have to work in the morning," he asked, later that afternoon, as we were getting back in my Tahoe to leave.

"Am I invited?"

"I think there's still ice cream in the freezer," Dawson said, and shrugged his shoulders.

"You had me at ice cream!" It was fun to banter with him. "Can we swing by my apartment real quick, so I can grab a few things?"

Easygoing Dawson didn't mind, and I grabbed a few things for work, and some fresh clothes. We spent the night together at Silver Shores, and I left the next morning before he woke up. I jotted a quick note and put it on the counter before heading to the hospital.

Kisha was ready for me when I got there, and the day was busy from the moment I stepped foot into the E.R. At some point in the day, my mom sent me a text asking for me to call her when I had the chance, but I wasn't in the mood, nor had the time to respond. She would have to wait a little to hear about the drama involving the boys in my love life.

Dawson sent me a message in response to my note that

was just a heart and it made my day better. Damn, I had fallen hard for him. A patient. Never in my life would I have thought I'd be going down this road. And especially with a guy who was a long-term relationship risk.

See you tonight? He messaged later in the afternoon.

Definitely, I get off at 7.

I was giddy he wanted me to come home to him and Kaleb happened to catch me as I was responding to his message.

"That smile wouldn't be the result of a good-looking pilot that we met a couple of weeks ago, would it?" he asked, and elbowed me.

"I have no idea what you're talking about..." He knew I was full of shit, but I could never admit to starting a relationship with a patient, especially in the hospital environment.

"I'm happy for you, Doc. Haven't seen a smile like this on your face in a while."

It was good to hear him say that. I hadn't felt quite so good in a while either.

The very idea of Dawson being in my life really made me want to settle down and make my career into more of what I had envisioned when I went to Med school. I wanted an office of my own where I could treat the whole patient and not just their eyes.

I made a mental note to talk to my father about it, even though I knew he would protest, because, "Emergency medicine is the best place to really help people." He had said it a thousand times.

But, I was finally in a place where I was ready to do my own thing. Hopefully, he would like my idea and help me find the resources to make it happen.

The road trip helped fuel my want for regular time off

too. I hadn't realized just how much I had been working.

No matter what happened in the days ahead with Dawson, it was time to do this for me...

CHAPTER FIFTY

The loud bang on the door told me all I needed to know.

Diana was here to clean my room.

"Come on in," I yelled from the bedroom where I was sorting laundry. I wondered if she had come by while we were on our road trip.

"Hello Mr. Clynes," she said from a distance. "The usual tidy up today, sir?"

"That would be great, but no vacuuming if you don't mind." I sat down on the bed and waited for her to make her way into the bedroom. When she finally did, I got a square look at her, exactly as I was hoping to do.

"So... Diamond... how long have you been working for Silver Shores?"

"Oh about a couple of weeks or so, still new..." she stopped and looked up, but wouldn't turn toward me. "Did you just call me Diamond?"

"Funny thing is... as my sight has improved, I started noticing you looked awfully familiar. It's a good wig, though, I'll give you that." Still dead in her tracks she stood. Not looking at me, not looking away, just standing. "Why did you and Bruno break into my condo?"

"Uhh, um…" I could see that the panic had set in.

"We're just talking here, no need to freak out, but I'd truly like to know why you broke into my condo? What exactly were you looking for?" I should have just called the cops, or at the very least, the Silver Shores manager on duty, and let them in on *Diana's* little secret.

She turned to face me, but again, still didn't say anything. I could hear the door open and close again. She must have signaled her *friend*.

"So, the pilot has figured us out, eh, Diamond?" Bruno said, as he walked into the room. Obviously, he had no lingering issues from our scuffle in the parking lot.

"I will ask you just like I asked her, what exactly do you want? Why did you break into my condo?" I wasn't scared of this motherfucker, but I was glad that Vixie was at the hospital and not here to witness whatever was about to go down.

"You see, Dawson, we needed to do a little gathering of information before we presented you with our offer. It just so happens that you figured out Diamond was in disguise before we stopped by this evening to discuss our plans with you," he said, and leaned against the doorway. I continued to sit with my feet propped up on the bed and the annoyed look on my face.

"Oh, you were?! That's a relief, I thought I was going to have to come find you. Would you get on with whatever it is?"

He walked around Diamond who was obviously a mere pawn in their relationship and sat down on the chaise. I didn't like the sight of him, much less his stench, in the condo.

"You see, Dawson. After lifting your social security number, date of birth, full name, etc., from the papers you left lying around... I was able to find out that you have a large sum of money sitting out there just waiting in the wings for you to do something with," he stopped. "And that something, is give it to me."

"*If* on God's green earth, AND THAT'S A BIG *IF*... If I did have a large sum of money just sitting somewhere, why in the world would I give it to you, Bruno?"

"Well, you'd give it to me, because I have the ability to ruin your career and your future, and all these people in Boca that you seem to love. I know all about your lady doctor friend. And your pilot buddy... followed him home the other night, he's got a nice place too... smokin' hot wife and cute kid... oh, and we can't forget your daddy? Know about him too. That's where most of your money goes, it seems. Paying his bills, even though he can't remember you from Adam. And Aunt Faye? She'd just be icing on the cake."

"You're insane!" I threw up my hands. "You can't blackmail me or threaten me when you have nothing to hold over my head."

"Oh, but I do, Dawson! I have witnesses who will testify that you came back to the bar once you healed up to attack me again over the embarrassment you had from the little black eye I gave you... and those witnesses, they'll make sure I look like you tried your best. See ya, pilot wings..." His words were infuriating. "And then all those people you love... they'll go for them. Not all at once, you see, but one by one, so it doesn't look suspicious. Antifreeze the kid's dog... pillow over your Pop's face, it'll look like it was his time to go... your sweet little doc might make it if they realize what the coffee-shop girl added to her coffee in time."

"You're fucking crazy! I don't have any money to give you! If I did, I would go to the ATM right now just to get you to leave us alone, you sick fuck!"

"That's exactly what I wanted to hear, Dawson! Good talk... it seems as if you're unaware that you have this large sum of money though, so I'll go ahead and share the paperwork with you..." He handed me a piece of paper with a bank name and an account number on it.

"You have until Wednesday to close that account and get me cash, and no cops... it will not end well for any of you if you involve the police," he said, and turned to Diamond. "Now finish cleaning his fucking room before you get fired."

CHAPTER FIFTY-ONE

There was something different about Dawson when I got to the condo that evening. He seemed troubled, and I assumed it was just him worrying over his vision improving.

"How was your day?" he asked, and came over to give me a kiss when I got in.

"It went fast today, which is good, but meant a lot of patients. I'm tired," I kissed him back and squeezed his shoulder.

"How was your day? You're still resting when you can, right? Doctor's orders are to continue to take it easy," I said.

"It was fine. I followed orders and chilled out today." He still seemed off. "Hey tomorrow...

Would you mind if I borrowed the Tahoe after my appointment? I have a few errands to run around town."

"That's fine, no problem. You want to just swing by and pick me up after my shift?"

"Yep, sounds great. Maybe we can go on a date?" I liked the sound of hoping his appointment went well and we'd be celebrating.

"I like dates."

"Good deal, it's a date then. Trip is going to drop me off for my appointment at eleven, so maybe I'll get to see you for lunch too."

"If I didn't know better, I'd say you had a *thang* for your doctor," I kissed him again and went to toss my stuff on the couch and take off my shoes. "My feet are tired today."

"More so than usual? How about I run you a hot bath and order dinner while you soak your piggies?" He pulled me against him and held me tight for a few seconds.

"Mmm, that sounds good, but I'd rather wait a bit and you join me?"

"Fast food, it is!" The smooth talker smiled and we decided to get tacos from down the street... fast, easy and good.

"I feel like there's something bothering you," I mentioned over dinner. I wondered if it was the future of our fling? Was it the fear of losing his career? Was it the fact that there was only one pint of ice cream left in the freezer and he was going to have to share it with me?

"Just tired, I suppose." Okay, so it wasn't the ice cream. And he was obviously not going to talk about it.

"Kaleb was working in the E.R. today," I said, changing the subject. "When I got your text earlier, he was teasing me that I was smiling like a schoolgirl at my phone, and wanted to know who I was crushing on."

"And did you tell him?" This got a smirk out of the pilot.

"I think he knew when I winked at him. It's not like I can go around telling coworkers I'm dating a hunky patient."

A phone call from Trip interrupted our conversation.

"Hey guys, back in town?" I heard him say when Dawson put the phone on speaker.

"Yep, we're back... hey, can you still run me over to the

hospital tomorrow around ten forty-five for my follow-up appointment?"

"Sure can, no problem. I can hang around too if you want."

"Vix is gonna let me borrow her Tahoe, so I'll be good if you can drop me off... got a few errands to run later in the afternoon."

"I wanted to see if y'all would be interested coming over for dinner tomorrow night?" Trip was ever the gracious host. Dawson looked at me for approval before saying anything and my face told him I didn't mind.

"We actually planned on going out... that barbecue place I like? You guys want to join us?"

"Hey, we could do that..." They talked for a little bit longer while I cleared the dishes and straightened up a bit.

I was most definitely interested in the bath Dawson mentioned earlier. I grabbed my body wash out of my travel case that I took on our road trip and went to run the water.

Bubbles were in our future.

"Hey, there, sight for sore eyes," I said, when I came into the exam room to find Dawson. I shut the door behind me and went over and kissed his cheek.

"Do all your patients get such excellent treatment?" he asked.

"Only the cute ones!" I washed my hands and put on a pair of gloves. "You've been doing good with your eye drops when I've been away. I'm proud of you."

"It's gotten easier over time," he admitted.

"The lubricating drops will come in handy for a while and I'd like to give you another prescription for an antibiotic drop that you'll continue for two more weeks. It's just a precaution and will help take care of you when you're back in the skies."

"If."

And there was the worry.

I knew it had been bothering him.

I gave him a quick examination with my pen light, and then sat him up in place against the phoropter, so I could get a good look at everything.

"These letters and symbols are going to be in a different order than your chart at the condo. So, take your time for me. We are in no hurry," I explained.

I did some research to find out the exact vision requirements Dawson would need to hit to keep his license. He needed 20/20 distant vision in each eye, 20/40 near vision in each eye, and 20/40 intermediate vision in each eye without correction, but could wear corrective lenses or contacts as long as he achieved 20/20 vision with their assistance. I never expected his injured eye to get back to 20/20, but I hoped and prayed he got to 20/40 on his own.

Dawson read off the symbols, told me where the items were in the house image, followed the dots and watched the flashes.

He did well.

"So here's the tough news," I said, turning the lights back up and scooting over next to him. "Your good eye is at 20/20. Fantastic vision. Your injured eye is at 20/40, so you will need a subtle prescription to get your sight down to 20/20. But that means you're still in the range to fly... right?"

He sank in my arms.

"Hey, there, hold up before you get emotional, I'm not done," I said, and I pulled his face to mine. "This is good, because your sight could still continue to improve over the next couple of weeks, too, and you may not need the glasses at all."

"I'll have to retest with the Aviation Medical Examiner before I'm cleared to fly again, but I was so worried that this first test wouldn't be good enough."

"Dawson, sweetheart... when do you ever disappoint?" The relief washed over both of us and I spent a little too much time with my patient in the exam room.

"And like no other sculpture in the history of art, the dead engine and dead airframe come to life at the touch of a human hand, and join their life with the pilot's own."

- *Richard Bach,*
A Gift Of Wings

CHAPTER FIFTY-TWO

The results of the eye exam were the hardest words I've ever waited to hear. The fact that they were relayed by the beauty before me made them a little easier to digest, and even though I still would have to get glasses, I couldn't have been more relieved.

We had celebratory pancakes for lunch, and I left her to go back to work and run *my errands*. Truth was, I needed to figure out what to do about Bruno. His bogus claim that I had a sum of money just sitting out there was mind boggling, but I had to check out the information he had given me.

Hell, I had never run any kind of search on myself to know. Why would I have ever needed to? But I figured if I made the effort to check it out, the least I could do was prove to him I had nothing that he'd want.

The safety of my friends and family weighed heavily on my mind as I pulled up to the chain establishment. It was a nationwide bank anybody would recognize, with branches in every major city I'd ever been to. I hoped there was someone who could assist me without an appointment. I wasn't even sure what to say when I got inside.

"Hello, sir, how may I help you," the portly teller asked with a smile.

"I'd like to speak to someone about an account? If there's someone available?" *Does it exist? Was this the right thing to say, or would that come off as a weird question?*

"No problem, sir. We have several bankers available." He directed me over to an area to wait a few minutes while someone came out to help me.

I made sure to bring several forms of ID with me, so if I had to prove *I was actually me* it wouldn't be a problem.

"Hi there!" A nice-looking lady in a purple suit said, as she came out of her office with large glass windows. "How may I help you today, sir?"

"Well," I said, as we walked into her space, and I sat down across the desk from her. She left the door open, which I thought was weird from a privacy standpoint, but also didn't see many people around for it to matter. "This is going to sound weird, however, I'm just going to come right out and ask and you can tell me what information you need."

"I'm ready," she said, and laced her fingers together over the cherry desk.

"A family friend of mine found an account number with your bank and claims that I may have had a sum of money set aside for whatever reason... I'd assume until I became a certain age... but I was never told about this account." *Wow, that came out awkward.*

"It's really not that weird at all, sir. Let me do a little searching and see what we can find. Do you have any form of ID with you today?" *Fancy you should ask, pat on the back for being prepared.*

I handed her the paper with the account number that Bruno had given me, along with my driver's license and passport. I figured that would be enough to identify me, since both had my picture. My license was still from Kentucky and had Aunt Faye's address listed on it, as I technically didn't live at the farmhouse any longer. She never mentioned any kind of mail or bank statements that had come to her house though, so the likelihood of the bogus money existing still was slim. Even if it did, how did it get there? Who deposited it?

"Okay, Mr. Kaczmarek," I appreciated her trying to pronounce my last name, even if she did butcher it. I rarely corrected people any more. "I do have an account here with your name and social. The address is different, is there another Kentucky address that you could have given us at some point in time?"

I rattled off my parents' old place to which she shook her head.

"Yep, that's what's showing here, and you do indeed have a balance. The account is currently a savings account, but I could transition it into a checking account if you need to make withdrawals."

"So it does exist?" I scratched my head.

"Indeed it does, sir. The account was opened roughly ten years ago, by a Colt Kaczmarek and has your name as the sole account holder... which means he could only deposit funds into it, he was unauthorized to withdraw."

"Colt is my dad... is it just one deposit? Does it say when . ten years ago it was made?" She turned the screen around, so I could view the information. My father had opened the account with a check from an insurance company a couple months after my mom passed away.

223

There really was a large sum of money just hanging out there waiting for me to find it.

CHAPTER FIFTY-THREE

Our celebratory "I could see!" dinner went well Monday evening and Tuesday and Wednesday were both normal work days for Vixie. Wednesday, however, was the day Bruno would be back, and after my time at the bank, I would be ready for him.

I wasn't going to put the ones I loved at risk because of some bully named Bruno. But, it wasn't like we had scheduled an appointment for him to swing by.

So I waited.

And waited.

And waited.

Bang, bang, bang. Ah, Diana. Or rather *Diamond*. I really hoped that mine was the only condo she visited.

"What can I help you with today, Mr. Clynes?" she asked, as she came inside rolling her cleaning cart.

"Cut the bullshit, Diamond. Where's Bruno?"

"It's not bullshit, this is actually my job. I clean and help out the residents of Silver Shores," she tried to explain.

"Oh, forgive me for assuming it was all a ruse. So, where

is he?" I didn't have the patience to deal with her playing dumb.

"He'll be here, I had to make sure I got in okay and the coast was clear," she said. "Want me to clean anything in the meantime?"

"I do need some towels," I said with annoyance. This whole situation had me pissed off. The sheer thought of me handing over money to this antagonizer was absolutely ridiculous.

A few minutes later, Bruno came in and closed the door behind him, just like the last time. I was sitting on the couch waiting while Diamond was cleaning the bathroom.

"So, do you have something for me?"

"We need to go over the terms again, just so it's all lined out and clear for me, and I understand completely," I ordered.

"You want me to tell you what I'm gonna do if you don't pay up? That's what you want to hear?"

"Yeah, I guess I do?" *Fucker, yes, I want to hear you say it.*

"Let me give you the short and sweet summary. Everybody that you love will suffer and all their blood will be on your hands."

"All this because of a little fight at a bar one night? I don't understand you, Bruno, *if that is your real name.*"

"No, that's just what got us introduced. This all because of that little pot of gold you have sitting in an untouched bank account. So let's get back to that..."

"How was it you were going to ruin my career again? That part is a little fuzzy..." I wasn't giving into him without at least an argument.

"Ha, I have a nice plan to go to the cops all beat up, and claim you assaulted me. That'll be good for your shiny pilot's license. Can't imagine they let people in jail fly planes."

"No, I can't imagine that they would."

"Your money is over there in that duffel bag," I pointed to the chair, where the bag was lying on the floor.

"Just like that? We have a little recap conversation and you hand it over to me? You pussy, that was easier than I thought it would be."

"Yeah, turns out the money was there, just like you said. I had no idea until you brought it to my attention, so it's not like I'll be missing anything. I just want my family and friends safe." I sat up in the chair. "And when you leave this condo, I don't ever want to see you again, do you hear me?"

I could have thrown down and beaten his ass, especially now that I was sober, but that wasn't part of the plan and would put the ones I loved in jeopardy again.

"I may not be a stand-up guy, but I'll keep my word," Bruno said. It made me want to vomit. Who would believe a word from this guy?

"Sure, you better keep your word." I waited for him to get the duffel, and told Diamond it was time for her to go, and that I wouldn't need *her specific* services anymore, whatsoever. I'd get my own towels from now on. I sent her packing before she even had a chance to say anything else to Bruno.

"The teddy bear for me too?" he said, as he reached down to pick up the bag, the stuffed animal sitting on the chair across from me.

"It's my nephew's," I said, waving at the bear. "Hi, Teddy!"

I stood there gawking at him, waiting for him to open the duffel.

He started to unzip the bag when we heard another bang on the door.

"Diana seriously needs to chill with the banging on the door, the people who live here are elderly."

I went over and opened the door, moving out of the way, so the officers could pass by me. Trip and company came in behind them.

"You're under arrest," was all I needed to hear, and Bruno would be out of our lives for a very long time.

Trip knew all the neighbors very well, so he and my princesses Muriel and Bertha were ready to act in the condo next door. The teddy bear that I said was my nephew's was Brucey's nanny cam, and Trip and the ladies were watching the live feed waiting for the right moment. His contact at the police station was onboard with letting our little plan play out, so long as I was the only one involved. I took the risk to put Bruno and Diamond away for good.

"Diana is already in cuffs in the cruiser outside," Trip said. "The nanny cam was a brilliant idea."

"Can't thank you enough for all your help. This wouldn't have worked without you." I reached my hand out and we did our secret pilot handshake for old time's sake.

"Twerrrrp!" we said simultaneously, as we turned the imaginary wheel and bumped fists.

Vixie was pulling up in her Tahoe as the officers were leaving with Bruno and Diamond.

"I've got some explaining to do..." I said.

"Yeah, I'll let you get to it," Trip said, and walked out with Muriel and Bertha at his sides. "Hey, Dawx? What was in the bag?"

"The duffel? Ha! Dirty towels from the bathroom..."

CHAPTER FIFTY-FOUR

After filling Vixie in on everything that happened with Bruno and Diamond, we spent the next two days regrouping, and anxiously awaiting my appointment with the Federal Aviation Association. She went with me to get glasses, and when I put them on we retested, several times, just to make sure my vision was 20/20. It was better than 20/20 when I had them on.

"I know I can't go in with you, but I will be right outside cheering you on," she said, and squeezed me tight. "You've got this, Dawx."

The FAA's test was even more rigorous than the practice tests we had done at the hospital, but I knew it would be. I felt good about how I did, and didn't have to wait long for my results. I left the exam room, and went down the hall with papers in hand that I had passed, and I could keep my wings.

She knew from the smile on my face before I even had to say a word that things were looking up.

"So, when do you fly out, Commander?" she asked. I

could see that she was happy for me, but a twinge of sadness peeked out from her eyes.

"Monday. Flight from Boca to JFK, then on to Beijing. Five-day trip and then back for two days."

"That soon, eh?"

"If my doctor releases me, of course." And that was a genuine concern. I wanted to make sure Vixie thought I'd do okay, before hitting this much elevation all at once. "I'll take the ride to JFK to make sure everything feels good, and then I'll sit in the First Officer position on the flight to and from. My supervisor wanted to meet after I got back in the air, to make sure I was okay before getting back in command. Makes sense to me."

"Your doctor will tell you that the elevation and pressure changes will cause headaches for a while, and it'll just have to be something you get used to, and treat with over-the-counter stuff like ibuprofen... but I think you're ready. When I did your procedure, I purposely did not use a gas bubble, knowing you'd need to get back in the air soon, and that would have been what caused you complications when you got up in the air. You'll know on the first flight to JFK if it's going to be too much for you." The disappointment in her voice was unmissable.

"Let's go get some ice cream, what do you say?" I'd bribe her as best as I could to find her smile, but this time, it didn't show—not even for ice cream. We started walking back to the car, and I put my arm around her to pull her closer to me.

"I knew life would go back to normal. I guess I just didn't expect to feel quite so empty inside." I didn't know what to say. What were we supposed to do? I just assumed we would continue to do life and see where things took us, but I felt empty too. "I've been talking to my father about opening my own practice."

I was pleased to hear her news, but wondered if this would drive us further apart, knowing she'd have to be busier than ever.

"That's good, right?"

"I think so, it's something I've wanted to do for a while. Mom and Dad are going to help me get it off the ground financially and help fill in for personnel, until I have a schedule and can hire someone else," she explained. She got in the passenger side of the Tahoe, expecting me to drive us home, wherever that might be. Home for me was starting to feel more like where she was than a physical place on a map.

I didn't drive home though. I drove to a local ice-cream parlor, as I previously suggested, and we both got two scoops in a waffle cone.

"It feels like we've been heading down this road for the last two weeks and we've finally arrived. The car is stopped. Here we are, and now... now what do we do?" She was saying all the words I had been thinking for a while.

"Why don't we take it one trip at a time? And just see? I don't want to leave on Monday and it *just* be over. That's not how this is going to go. It can't be." I choked myself up at the thought of a clean break.

"But what happens when you come home and I have to work? We see each other for a few hours and then off you go again?" It was not ideal, not at all. We both knew that.

"Let's just get through this first trip. Please, Vixie. When I get back next Friday, I'll be off for two days before something else."

"Okay... okay. We can think about it over the next week and talk about it when you get back. I just know that I can't constantly wonder when or if I'm going to get to see you again," she said, and finally took a bite of her ice cream.

"I know... I can't either."

Riding as a passenger from Boca to JFK felt like I was sailing on clouds. I hadn't realized how much I missed being in the air. The next step was getting back in the cockpit. Nonstop flights were my favorite and this one was just under three hours. No pain whatsoever, and no headache... at least not yet.

I had a little bit of a layover in New York before the long flight to Beijing, and managed to catch Vixie on her lunch break, so that was most definitely a win.

The next flight was fifteen hours. As First Officer on most short flights, the pilot rarely gave up command, but when flights were this long, the captain always needed a couple of breaks. It was a good way to get back in the saddle.

"Your glasses look good, sir," Cammie said, when she came in the cockpit to tell us the passengers were on board and ready to taxi. She was one of the flight attendants I flew with regularly. "Like a sexy librarian."

"Funny, that's exactly the look I was going for..." Vix would get a kick out of that comment. I was able to message her using apps on my phone when we were in the air and able to connect to Wi-Fi. I felt good about having that little connection even if it wasn't immediate.

By the time we arrived in China, my eyes were so tired. I had forgotten to put the lubricating drops in when I took a break, and needed to remember to do that in the future.

"Wanna grab a drink?" Cammie asked as we were departing.

"Nah, I'm tired tonight, gonna head to the hotel." I was not going to push it by trying to be social. Not yet anyway. I knew I needed to rest.

I sent Vixie a message, knowing she'd be asleep and wouldn't get it until morning her time. I wanted her to know I missed her, even though we had only been apart for a couple of days.

God, I *really* missed her.

"If you were born without wings,
do nothing to prevent them from growing."

-Coco Chanel

CHAPTER FIFTY-FIVE

"There's just so much competition here in Boca, why not look elsewhere... smaller towns nearby?" My father's suggestion was to be smart about opening my own practice, and to do it specifically where there was a need. He wasn't wrong, but the thought of moving elsewhere just didn't feel right.

"I'll do some research. We don't have to decide anything today."

I spent the evening with them after work on Tuesday, desperately missing Dawson, knowing I had gotten myself way too attached too soon, and I was on my way to mending a broken heart.

"Just because your new boyfriend isn't in town at the moment, doesn't mean you need to work yourself to death, dear." Ah, mother. My schedule was full, not because of Dawson, but because of the nature of my job. Yet another reason I wanted to have my own place, so I could control my own hours.

I miss you. His message came through in the middle of the night when I got back home.

Oh, how I miss you too, Dawx. I didn't want to feel like this all the time, but I couldn't ask him to give up everything to just sit in my apartment while I worked. The very thought of it was dumb, and vice versa. He'd never ask that of me either.

As he was moving out of Trip's condo, I suggested he leave a few things at my place. His swim trunks, for one thing. He wouldn't be needing them in Beijing. He also left his hoodie, which I had on every minute I was in my apartment. I couldn't get enough of his smell.

Kendall and I had struck up a friendship, which I enjoyed. We talked about all things Boca, coffee—which she also loved—and hunky pilots. She and Trip had a little different beginning than me and Dawson, but she said they just knew at one point they no longer wanted to be apart.

I felt that in my soul.

Zak had messaged me a couple times, which I ignored, and finally told Denny to pass along the word that I was no longer interested.

At home, I wallowed in Dawson's hoodie, and decided I'd just go to bed early, knowing I'd have a long workday ahead of me. I opened the bottom drawer of my dresser where I told Dawson he could put his things and found his swim trunks right where he had left them. My favorite mental image of him taking his shirt off at the pool and watching the trunks creep down his hips came to mind. I wanted to make that memory permanent.

Before I closed the drawer back, I noticed something sticking out of his pocket.

"Found this when you were swimming in the ocean. I never want to forget that day," the note read. And after further digging in his pocket, I found a pink seashell that slightly resembled the shape of a heart.

Oh Dawson, I never want to forget that day either.

Friday night couldn't come too soon. I was excited to be able to get off work and go pick Dawson up from the airport. I was thrilled that the first time we were away from one another, our schedules actually lined up. I had to work Saturday, but had plans to spend the entire day with him Sunday, just enjoying each other. *Maybe, maybe we* could *make this work.*

The inevitable looming of what was to come still hung in the back of my mind. His messages indicated his eye felt okay on flights, even through the turbulence and pressure changes, and his headaches were minimal. I was so glad to hear that.

I parked and decided to go inside to pick him up once he made it past security. I didn't plan on doing that every time, but I felt like this was a special occasion. It had been less than a week and *I was aching to see him.*

There were strangers there with signs for their passengers, welcoming them home, and I thought about how I could have showed up with a sign. Welcome home, Commander. His flight time showed it was early and he had already landed when I found a place inside to wait for him. I thought about what it looked like watching him fly a plane and knew it was a sight.

Thank goodness I wouldn't have to wait very long. Person after person came through and I knew I just had to have patience. The crew was always last to exit the plane.

When I could finally see him turn the corner, way off in the distance, his captivating stare bewitched me. It was like I could read his thoughts and feel his emotions as he walked down the long stretch of carpet toward me. The pilot's suit didn't hurt either. It fitted perfectly and hugged all the right places. The four gold captain's stripes on his jacket added a level of seriousness that I wasn't used to seeing on him. Even though he hung back and wasn't in command this trip, I wanted that back for him.

It seemed like hours as he walked toward me, pulling his suitcase behind him, but the whole time we never looked away. Once our eyes locked, though. That was it. He was on autopilot to get to me.

"Evening, Doctor," he said, when he was almost through the security barrier.

"Evening, Commander... need a ride?"

"Oh, I need more than a ride," he said, as he finally passed through the barriers, sliding off his captain's hat and pulling me into him. Dawson kissed me like we had been apart for a decade. I couldn't help but worry the feeling of him being gone would creep back up come Monday. And this time it could be a longer stretch.

"This suit of yours..." I said, catching my breath. "It looks fantastic on you... I can't wait to see it on my apartment floor."

"Oh, no, ma'am. We'll take a minute to hang it up... make the foreplay last a little longer," he teased. He didn't let go of me, despite the onlookers, and finally rubbed noses and kissed my cheek. "You, ma'am, are a sight."

"Have I told you how good you look in glasses?" I asked, as we started to walk away.

"No, but I recently heard they make me look like a librarian."

CHAPTER FIFTY-SIX

What's that old saying, absence makes the heart grow fonder?

It wasn't lying. When I saw her in the airport, my heart sank. God, I missed her.

I'd had a lot of time to think in the air on the way and back to China.

And I had a plan.

And a free Saturday to do it.

She had to work her usual schedule and I was able to convince Trip to cart me around town.

Dinner out, or dinner in? I sent her a message. If she wanted to eat at her apartment, I had some grocery shopping to do, unless she wanted to split the one Lean Cuisine that was still left in the freezer.

Out. No cleaning this weekend. Then I can have you all to myself. I liked the way she thought.

Sounds great, I already have an idea. Pick me up at Trip's?

When we got done running around, I went back and hung out with him and Brucey that afternoon until Vixie got off work. It felt good just having a *normal* Saturday after-noon. I had taken for granted what that felt like.

"Hey, guys," she said, as she rolled down the window in the Tahoe. "Ready to go, Dawx?"

I was indeed ready to go, as she was too. It seemed pretty obvious she was not planning on staying for a minute.

"Yes, ma'am," I said, and ran my fingers through Brucey's hair, annoying him like a good uncle would. "Later, Trip. See ya, Kendall."

"See you Tuesday for coffee," Vix said to Kendall as well. It was nice seeing they had made a friendship. I hopped in the Tahoe and gave orders.

"I want to go to that little seafood place not far from your parents and take a stroll on the beach after we're done eating," I suggested. "That sound okay?"

"It sounds like I don't have to decide and I love it!"

We feasted on fresh seafood and had a couple drinks to go along with dinner, not enough to make either of us tipsy, or mess with my nerves. I was anxious to get on the beach and reveal my plan. We slid our shoes off and tossed them in the vehicle, before heading out on the sand to watch the sunset.

"I'm just going to be completely honest with you, Vix..." She turned her head up toward me and I could see a little worry on her face. "The past five days felt lonely. I missed the heck out of you. And what's crazy about it... what I thought would just be a fling, and we'd go our separate ways... has completely surprised me, and made me want to never leave your side."

"Yeah... I didn't expect what we had in the beginning to be more than just a little fun, and then you'd fly off, and I'd go back to my usual every day," she stopped for a second, "but it's not just a fling, is it?"

No, baby, it's not.

I got serious for a second. "As you know, I have recently become aware of a sum of money that I have at my disposal," I tried not to laugh, as did she, "And I think fate put that money away from me for a reason... *the right reason.*"

"Already burning a hole in your pocket?" she teased. I grabbed her hand and laced our fingers together.

"Do you remember the one thing my dad said to me when we first saw him, and he had a moment where he was his old self? *'I want you to find somebody that will make you happy. Happy like your mama made me.'*" I gulped. "Vixie, that's you. You make me happy like my mom made my dad. Maybe even more so."

We kept walking as the sun was disappearing on the horizon. A shell scratched under my foot and I stopped to pick it up. It was a pink shell, almost resembling a heart, like the one I found the day we came to swim.

"Know how we'd make fun of Trip for selling out and becoming a family man?" I asked, having told her stories of how the other pilots teased him.

"Yep."

"Truth is, I'm envious of him, and I didn't know it until *you* happened, but I desperately want what he has. So, let me just say this before I lose my nerve, and then you can tell me how you feel..."

I explained to her that earlier in the day, I had interviewed for a contract pilot position for the private jet company where Trip worked, and they offered me a job on the spot. Just like him, they would allow me to choose when I wanted to work. Specifically, they flew direct out of both Boca Raton, Florida, and Louisville, Kentucky. The offer was the best of both worlds, I would still be able to fly, but on my own terms, and pick and choose my own schedule.

"Dr. Trevelian, the jolly old eye doctor who owns an optometry center back home, is retiring and closing up shop. I am ready to put an offer on his place with the equipment included if you're willing to move. I'm sure there would be some improvements you'd want to make, of course, but the place would be yours to do with what you like," I said and took a deep breath.

We stopped walking and Vixie turned toward me. I could see a couple tears had fallen down her cheeks and I hated the fact that I had made her cry. I knew it was all too much at once. But the pieces had to align perfectly or I knew we wouldn't be able to make it.

I handed the shell to her, the mate to the shell I had hidden in her bottom drawer.

"It's a big decision, but if you want this... *us*... *this future*, I'm ready to give it to you, no questions asked," I said. "There's an old farmhouse for rent back in Kentucky too... I think I could persuade the owner to let us buy it and make it a home." A home. *Our home.*

"While you were gone, I met with my parents about potentially opening my own practice," she said. My heart sank a little bit. "I swear, my father suggested I find someplace else to do it... a place with a need. He was right, of course, I just thought he was crazy. Why would I move from this gorgeous place that has everything I love?"

She squeezed me tightly and pulled the other shell from her pocket, handing it to me, putting the two together. "I've been carrying this shell around in my pocket all week. Wearing your hoodie. Wishing away time until you were back. I know now I just want to be where *you* are.

"So we're doing this?" I had to know for sure she wanted this future...

"I'll follow you anywhere, Dawson Kaczmarek."

"You know you had me when you pronounced my name that night in the hospital, right?"

"You had me when you asked me if it was possible you were pregnant like a male seahorse..."

"You are the pilot of your life.
So fly through the sky."

– *Angel Moreira*

EPILOGUE

Six Months Later

The tavern in Spring City was the perfect place for Dawson's bachelor party. Trip had wrangled all his friends to find a weekend for a nice, long layover, and they all made it to town to celebrate my captivating commander.

Aunt Faye sold the farmhouse to us at a steal, and we had been working on remodeling the place Dawx had grown up into our *own home*. We gutted a lot of the appliances, put in new floors, set up a library—my father taught me well—and began digging up the backyard for a pool. It was the one thing I told Dawson I would miss from Florida, swimming. So he was making an in-ground, heated pool and whirlpool happen.

Being close to Dawson's father was nice too. I made sure to go see him at least once a day during the week. I could walk over and say hello, and make sure he was getting a little people interaction. Some days he recognized me, most days he didn't. But, he always called me his cute doctor, and I wouldn't miss those sentiments for anything.

The coffeehouse in town and ice-cream shop were my safe havens. I passed by them and tried new things on my daily walks. The garden tub at the farmhouse made all four of my weaknesses easily accessible. Coffee. Ice Cream. Bubble baths. And, Dawson shirtless in swim trunks. That was most definitely my fourth weakness. All of which I could have whenever I wanted.

It had taken some time to buy the place, fix it up and evaluate needs, but my practice was about to open. I worked out a business and marketing plan, and purchased all the updates for the old equipment I had acquired. The town was in need of an eye-care center, as folks were currently travelling to Louisville and Lexington for good eye care, and it would be a place where I could care for my patients, not just get them in and out as fast as possible, or move on to the next emergency.

With my parents being retired, they found a condo nearby they rented out, and decided they liked the idea of being snowbirds. They could easily hop on board with Dawx any time they wanted, and travelled to and from Boca regularly. Dad had been crucial in making sure I got the business off to a good start, and Mom was thrilled at the idea of playing receptionist at the center.

The bell on the door jingled, telling me someone had arrived as I was putting together an office chair. I peeked out to see it was Dawson, checking in as he often did in the afternoon. The pitter patter of puppy claws against the tile came rushing toward me as well.

"Hey guys!" I said, reaching down to pick up our puppy. Dawson was second to get kissed after our new dachshund pup, eloquently named Hound, covered me with kisses. Together they were my Dawx Hound boys.

"Talked to Trip? Have the pilots arrived yet?" I asked.

"Yep, they landed a little bit ago. Should be here in about an hour."

"Are you excited to see your friends?" I already knew the answer.

"Yep, I'll try to refrain from bar fights though... the last time that happened, I wound up in the emergency room."

"The last time that happened, you found me," I teased. Dawson's sight had continued to improve and he rarely wore his glasses unless he was flying. It was still cute though, he looked studious when he wore them, and if it was possible... even sexier.

Getting out of everyday emergency medicine had changed me a little bit. I missed the hustle and bustle, not knowing what was coming in the door and how to help them, until they were in my capable hands. But seeing the faces of the residents in town as they welcomed us, and knowing I would be able to make a difference in their everyday lives felt like it would be so rewarding.

"Kendall will be here too," Dawson said, surprising me.

"No! She came all this way?" Kendall had become one of my dearest friends. For the few weeks we were in Boca before making the move north, we were practically inseparable. She had already gone through all this with Trip and had the best advice. Plus, we loved the same things. It was nice having a gal pal to share life with.

"Yes, she did. I'd go out on a limb and say she might have been more excited to come than Trip," he said and laughed. "Is the place going to be ready for the ribbon cutting and official opening next week?"

"Sure is," I said, if I can get the last few things put

together. I tossed up my hands at the office chair and let him take over.

We planned our wedding a few months out, so I wouldn't have to close up shop immediately once the center was opened. My parents would be on hand the whole time too. I just wouldn't have any eye appointments while we were gone on our honeymoon. Later, I would see if the center's income would warrant another ophthalmologist, like me.

"We haven't talked about what we want to do for our honeymoon, yet... any ideas?"

"Baby, I'll fly you anywhere you want to go," Dawx said, and swung me around in his arms.

"Love, I know that, but where is what I'm wondering about..."

"You think about it, I'm happy as long as I'm with you, so I'll let you decide."

"That's what I want for our honeymoon...to see you fly. Can I be your second in command?" The request caught him off guard.

"Hmm, I don't think you can be my second in command, but I might be able to sneak you in the third seat of the cockpit. Would you like that?"

"Can I wear your Captain's hat?"

"Yes, ma'am," he said, and rolled the chair over to me and Hound. "You still have to figure out where we're going though."

"I hear Florida is nice this time of year..."

I was too excited to get home and hang out with Kendall to think about the honeymoon. I grabbed my keys and headed out to lock up the center. The idea of watching Dawson fly hadn't left my mind since the first time I saw him in his full uniform.

"This bachelor life of yours… it's soon coming to an end, eh?" I said to Dawson as we headed to the Tahoe. The next item on our to-do list would be to get Dawx his own vehicle now that we were settled.

"You know, the life of a bachelor really suited me, until I met you. Now I'm ready to leave that in the past and keep hanging out with my favorite doctor. *Doctor Wifey* has a nice ring to it." I looked down at the diamond he had placed on my hand several weeks before.

"*Commander Hubby* has a nice ring to it too," I said, and grabbed the puppy's leash. "Ready to go home, Hound? Your papa's got a date with some *playboy pilots!*"

COCKY HERO CLUB

Want to keep up with all of the new releases in Vi Keeland and Penelope Ward's Cocky Hero Club world? Make sure you sign up for the official Cocky Hero Club newsletter for all the latest on our upcoming books:

https://www.subscribepage.com/CockyHeroClub

Check out other books in the Cocky Hero Club series:
http://www.cockyheroclub.com

ACKNOWLEDGMENTS

A huge thank you to Vi and Penelope...it has been an absolute pleasure working with you. Thank you for allowing me to play in your world and use your characters. I am humbled and honored to be a part of this project.

My sincerest thanks to Dan Piedade, Ann Atwood, Keri Simpson, Maylyn Carby, Megan Damrow, Lorah Jaiyn, Laura Finley, Bryan Harrell, David Stone, Tricia Radford, Megan Sevier, Tommy Huelsman, Whiskers & Words and Facebook friends for answering my random questions and helping me build this story.

OTHER BOOKS BY TIFFANY CARBY

www.tiffanycarby.com

Standalones/Anthologies

Recarpeting, A short, non-fiction narrative

To Grammy's House We Go *(Company of Griffins story)*

Art Inspires Words: Book Two *(Company of Griffins story)*

Jesse's Bar

Murder Maker

Tucker in Time

Hell-come to Crazy Town

The Dog's House

Children's Books by Tiffany & Sara Sokolowski

The Artistic-Zany Monster Family

Mino Penguin's Beach Birthday

Mamaw Tiger Just Wants a Nap

Ms. Lizards Lesson on Lemons

Made in the USA
Columbia, SC
05 November 2021

48418078R00159